ANTHOLOGY

A Timeless Anthology

TIMELESS ANTHOLOGY

Table of Contents

<u>Young Talent Showcase</u>

I am passionate about the horror literature industry and raising the next generation of readers, authors and artists in the genre. I have vowed to showcase the work of young talent in all my work going forward; to show them that their passions and talents are both valid and important.

The following piece of art was made specifically for this anthology by Brayden H. from Green Bay, Wisconsin. I found out about his amazing knack for art through his father, Sam. I am grateful for their kindness and support, and I'm honored to share his art with the world!

About the Artist:

Brayden is a 12-year-old homeschooler from Green Bay, Wisconsin. He is passionate about creating things and loves to spend his free time drawing, writing short stories and making stop motion videos.

Introduction

Inevitably, things change throughout time. That's just a part of life. There have been different trends in fashion, food, societal beliefs, and so on. For as long as people have been alive, though, one thing has never changed: There has always been *something* to be afraid of.

Whether we were afraid of wild animals or other predators, mankind, creepy crawlies, the monster under the bed, or the shadows that lurk. The fear of dying alone, the fear of drowning, the fear of the number 7…the list goes on and on. One thing that has never changed, and never will change, is that horror is timeless.

Through the next 9 stories, you will see that horror will never truly go away. It's in our nature as human beings on this earth to have an innate fear of *something.* So, clutch your pearls and pull your covers tight because for the rest of this book… well, I can't promise what's beyond this page.

1. Cody

Jared Grace (1800's)

The sound of Annabelle's feet crunching on the dry dirt outside her bedroom window startled the chirping crickets, casting the night into total silence. She squatted down and held her breath, ears tuned to any sound that might indicate her parents, specifically her father, had heard her escape. She could hear the blood pumping behind her ears and taste the acrid saliva pooling in her mouth as she closed her eyes and hoped the sound of her feet wouldn't travel far.

Her parents' home, set just outside downtown Cody, Wyoming, sat atop a small rise–nothing compared to the massive peaks that shadowed the distant horizon but high enough that she could see the dim lights flickering at The Lonesome Wolf Saloon. The distant sounds of laughter and raised voices carried over the silent night and draped themselves upon her like a spider's web over a fly.

If I can hear them from this far away, surely Pa can hear me just behind these wooden boards, she thought as her heart sank lower, her eyes darting back and forth from the door to the town below. She closed her eyes in an attempt to calm her nerves, and when the first cricket began chirping again, she allowed herself the comfort of opening them.

Several minutes passed.

With no sound of her father's heavy footsteps approaching her room, or worse yet, the front door, Annabelle allowed herself to rise from her crouched position and move quickly away from her home. She clutched her dress around her thighs and hefted it up above her ankles, careful not to trip as she made her way past the Viburnum shrubs and onto the dirt path that would lead her into town and eventually out to the large hackberry tree that stood sentry on the opposite side.

She could already imagine her love sitting beneath its branches, watching the town closely for any sign of her approach. She imagined him with his blue shirt on, the top two buttons open to reveal a soft patch of brown hair. His denim jeans, dirty on the knees and backside as he rested in the dirt…waiting.

She thought of his father's Colt pistol on his hip.

Annabelle looked at the moon's location and knew it must be getting close to midnight. She saw an ominous red light, hanging by the white moon. It moved slowly, but purposely. Worry crossed her face as she feared being late. Not that he would mind, but the later she was, the sooner she'd have to bid him farewell and slink back to her home, not knowing when she'd see him again.

She knew it was risky to sneak out of Pa's house. She had been warned of what happens to young girls when they disobey their father's directions. The evil, both human and otherwise, that lurks in the darkened corners of the world.

It was that very morning while she was out shopping with her Ma that she overheard a conversation between two cowboys about a creature that was lurking in the area. A creature that stole upon sheep and young women alike. And, really, Annabelle thought, is a young woman much different than a helpless sheep?

Moonlight shone off the quartz stones at her feet, reminding her of the gleam of her love's pistol when he wielded it in defense of a child who had stumbled into the wrong store at the wrong time.

The poor child was stunned when a man with a

bandana covering his nose and mouth turned, gun in hand, and pointed it at him. Annabelle had been in the corner of the store hiding and hoping the whole horrible event would end, when the man that would soon become her love followed the boy in.

Though she had yet to formally meet the man, she was instantly smitten by his looks and bravery. Her heart raced when his pistol was suddenly gripped in his calloused hand; she had never seen a gun drawn so quickly. She was so mesmerized by it that she hardly registered the BANG as the bullet left the pistol and hammered its way into the would-be robber's skull.

The young boy dropped to the ground in surprise. Annabelle rose, a smile wide on her face. The wispy tendrils of smoke passed by her hero's eyes as he twirled the pistol and slid it back into its holster in one smooth motion.

When Annabelle rushed toward him, his hand instinctively reached for the gun once more before registering that there was no threat. No other would-be robber was lurking in the back of the store, just a perky, young girl rushing forward with a smile that could block out the sun.

"Th-that was amazing!" Annabelle breathlessly spoke as she grasped her hands to her chest. "I've never seen anything like that before."

The cowboy tipped his cap and lowered his head. "I hope you never have to see anything like that again, ma'am."

He turned to leave the store, but Annabelle clutched at his arm and urged him to turn to her once more. She had only sipped the sweet nectar of his eyes momentarily, and she needed to sate her thirst fully before he walked out of her life.

When he turned, he kept his eyes low, the shadow of his hat darkening the windows to his soul. Annabelle bent low, a smile still spread across her face. She risked bringing one hand below his chin, softly urging him to raise his head and stare into her as she wished to stare into him.

The man shifted slightly, his weight changing from his right leg to his left; his spurs clinked softly as he did.

"Ma'am, please…" the man started.

"It is impolite to not gaze upon a lady who wishes for your attention." Annabelle had never been so bold and if her mother had been close by, she likely would not have been then either. But, she was alone with him at that moment. He raised his eyes and looked at her. Truly took her in as his crystal blue orbs flicked back and forth over her hazel ones.

Suddenly, the man's eyes looked past her and widened. Annabelle feared the robber was not truly dead and could imagine the heat of a bullet passing through her body, chipping bones and tearing through muscle. Her legs went momentarily weak and she feared she would fall into his strong, tanned arms. However, modesty won the moment, and she caught herself before the man even noticed her sway.

The cowboy simply moved to the side of Annabelle cautiously and took several determined steps past her.

When his eyes unlocked from hers it was as though the world came back into focus. She heard the soft sobs of the child behind her. The cowboy walked over and knelt before the young boy. He raised the boy's chin, not unlike what Annabelle had attempted to do moments before to him. The boy inhaled deeply and breathed out all the air he had in his lungs in an attempt to calm himself.

The cowboy glanced over his shoulder before leaning in close to the young boy. He whispered something to him, softly in each ear, and stood back up. The young boy watched him as he rose to his full height, a shadow now cast over the child. The boy made himself stand erect and tightened his face. He reached out to the cowboy with an anticipating hand

and clutched the calloused hand of the man who had saved his life.

The boy glanced at the pool of blood that had encircled his shoe, stepped calmly away from it, and made his way out of the store without a glance back over his shoulder.

"What did you say to him?" Annabelle asked in wonder.

The cowboy turned to face the young woman and smiled. "I told him that God was with him today. I told him that he walks with the Lord's holy light shining down upon him. I told him he will always be protected."

Annabelle's mouth hung open. "You are a man of God? But, you just killed a man."

The cowboy held a finger up gently and corrected her. "I killed an evil man doing the devil's work. I killed to save an innocent. If there had been another way I would have taken it. I always do."

She watched him as his eyes drifted to scenes that she could only imagine. His rugged exterior seemed to melt before her eyes, softening his features and somehow making him even more beautiful than he was before.

She reached out and took his hand, another bold move that would have made her mother gasp. He snapped back to the present and offered a slight smile and a light squeeze of her hand.

"Mister, thank you," the store clerk offered as he finally rose from behind the counter.

The cowboy tipped his hat and walked out the door.

When a drunken man stumbled out of The Lonesome Wolf Saloon, arms wrapped around his friends, Annabelle was brought back to the crunching ground beneath her feet. Her heart leaped with the sudden appearance of the men and the ear-shattering shouts coming from the drunk being carried out.

"Ah, fuck you, Willy. I'm totally fine. Sober as a judge," the man in the middle slurred just before leaning over and wretching all over his boots.

The stench was immediate as Annabelle had to sidestep the warm whiskey, steak chunks, and bile that splashed just short of where she had been walking. She immediately put her hand to her nose and turned her head in disgust. The two more sober men didn't notice her elusive move, but the drunkard did.

"What do we have here, men?" the man sneered as he wiped a shirt sleeve across his face. "Looks like the night has just begun."

Annabelle did her best to ignore the men and continue on her way. She could see the hackberry tree's silhouette projected on the sparse landscape. She knew her love was there. She imagined seeing him, one foot against the tree, his hat lowered over his eyes. Her heart began to race as she heard the men behind her once more.

"Hey, girl. We ain't gonna hurt'cha. We just wanna talk to ya," said the drunk. Annabelle swore she smelled his putrid breath as he got closer.

"Thank you, gentlemen. I'd love to stay and talk, but I have a date with my love. He's right over there by that hackberry tree. I really must be going." Annabelle thought that if she spoke gently and explained that she would be meeting with her man that these men may leave her alone. For just a moment she allowed herself to breathe easier as she heard the men's footsteps stop. She picked up her pace slightly and kept her eyes focused on the hackberry tree, her safety.

She only heard the rustling of feet for a fleeting moment before she was struck in the back of the head. Her world spun as her head hit the dirt road in the center of town. Her eyes wouldn't focus and her breath came out in short, ragged gasps. She managed to roll onto her back, desperate for someone who had seen the attack to come to her aid.

But the street was quiet at this time of night. The crickets chirped in the distance, an owl hooted, and Annabelle's eyes began to close with the sight of three blurry men standing above her. As her vision tunneled she saw the drunk man, vomit still mixed into his beard, lean close.

"It's better you're asleep for this, girl. Pray you don't wake up."

Annabelle opened her eyes to the beautiful sun and a gentle breeze running through her hair. Her head was in her love's lap, his eyes once more cast down but this time staring deeply into hers.

The breeze died down suddenly and his fingers took up the light caressing of her hair. She had snuck out several times before, always at night, but this time she risked her parent's wrath and crawled out her window just after lunch when she knew her parents would nap for at least a couple hours.

She thought about the first time they met, when her love saved the child in the nick of time. Annabelle had followed him out of the store and asked to meet him the next night. The cowboy sighed deeply, took her hand, and agreed to meet her under the hackberry tree the following night at midnight. She sat up that night unable to calm the butterflies in her stomach but giddy with excitement.

The next night, and every other encounter since, he had been a perfect gentleman. Even when she risked leaning forward one night, expectantly with pouty lips, he did no more than kiss her cheek and tell her she was the most perfect woman he'd ever been around.

He was a killer, but he was a man of God, and had Christian expectations to uphold as well. He would make her his, and then he would be able to kiss those lips and, Annabelle hoped, do a lot more.

Annabelle stretched her arms over her head and let out a deep sigh–one of utter relaxation. The backs of her fingers gently touched the grip of his pistol; she had never touched a gun before and she dared not move now in fear that it might go off.

Sensing her sudden tension, her love lightly blew air from his nose and placed his hand over hers. The weight of his hand pushed hers into the grip harder, and her breath caught. The man took her hand and placed it on her stomach before reaching back and unholstering the weapon. She watched him from her periphery as he held it up to the sky, sunshine glinting off the polished metal, and placed it beside her hand, rising and falling with each breath.

"Go on, pick it up." His voice was soft but firm. A direction for her to follow but not an order.

"I-I've never held a gun before. I don't want it to fire."

"Well, the good news is it won't if you only hold it here." He placed the grip in her open hand and pointed it off into the distance. "See? Perfectly safe if you know what you're doing."

Annabelle rose to a sitting position, confidence and exhilaration coursing through her, and tested its weight as she moved it from side to side. She pointed it at the bushes, and trees in the distance, and was startled to realize that she was pointing it at a small ground squirrel some distance away.

She lowered the gun back into her lap and sighed.

"It's powerful. So powerful. To hold the key to life and death in the palm of your hand. Why do you do it?"

The man picked the gun up from her lap and holstered it once more. He sat quietly for a few moments before removing his hat, placing it at his side, and turning to face her.

"I take no pride in taking a life. That is not why I carry this gun. You see…it was my father's gun."

"Was?"

The man nodded slowly.

"He was a preacher way over in Laramie, where I'm from. He was a good man. A hard-working, honest man." The cowboy paused, contemplatively. He ran his fingers over the blades of grass as he thought about how to continue.

"When some of his congregation began to talk about creatures that stalked their homesteads, killing animals and making all sorts of devilish noises in the moonlight, he took it as a sign of things to come. These were no Indians and they weren't no common bandits, he knew. He prayed to God each night for guidance. How could he protect the congregation and, most importantly, his own family?

"The next day there was a heavy knock on our door. My father rushed to it and flung it open to find dozens of women and several men on their knees, begging for help. One of the women had watched a…monster take her child in the dawn hours that very morning."

"A monster? She must have been mistaken," Annabelle said breathlessly.

"I fear not. She claimed it was around eight feet tall

with fingers longer than most men's forearms. She said its hair hung low, covering its face, but she could see that it had the body of a woman. There was a stench that came with it–like rotting flesh and corrupted earth."

Annabelle allowed herself a soft giggle as she stared into the man's eyes.

"You're just trying to scare me," she said as she placed her hand on his knee.

"I wish that were true. But I have since seen one."

Annabelle's mouth fell open as she sat back waiting for him to continue.

"That morning my father went out and bought this pistol. He aimed to hunt this creature and, if possible, save the young child that was taken. When he left that night, I had begged to go with him. I was only fifteen at the time, but I couldn't justify sitting at home waiting for his return…doing nothing. My father would hear nothing of it. As I watched him ride his horse out into the oncoming darkness, I wondered if I'd ever see him again.

"That night was one of the strangest of my life. The noises my mother and I heard outside–the noises we told ourselves were just the wind–chilled us to the bone. The air felt heavy and stale. The owls stayed quiet that night.

"Then suddenly, three gunshots rang out. It was hard to tell how far away they were, sound carried funny out there, but we suspected they were close. We rushed to the window and watched for any sign of my father, but we saw nothing. An hour later, though it felt like it could have been days, we saw his torch break the tree line at the edge of our property. Mother ran out onto the porch and called his name. I followed, watching for something I knew was there but could not see.

"As he got closer I could see that he was hurt. His shirt was torn from chest to stomach, a bloody gash traced its way down toward his belly button. But, he was smiling."

'I got it, son. I killed the demon!' he called out as he got closer.

"When Mother noticed the state of him, she rushed into the house to fetch some clothes and water. He hobbled up to the porch with eyes that showed he had seen the depths of hell itself. The smile now seemed to be frantic.

"That's when the screech cut through the air. In an instant, it had leaped from the rooftop, cat-like, and was on top of my father, tearing at his throat and his chest. Pulling his insides out and tossing them into the dirt. Blood splattered onto my shirt and face. I was horrified. My father didn't even know what happened. I guess that is one of God's blessings."

"Oh…oh that's horrible." Annabelle cried as she shifted herself closer to her hero. "Are…are you sure it wasn't an animal? As awful as it is, perhaps it was simply hunting."

He placed his arm around her and pulled her into him.

"Oh, it was hunting. But, it was no animal. Before it ran off, it turned to me. The dark hair covered its eyes but the sharp, jagged teeth were covered in gore. Its breasts heaved with excitement. I swear it was smiling.

"I was frozen until it was out of sight. Why it didn't attack me, I'll never know. Somewhere in the back of my mind, I heard my mother scream. I paid it no mind. I slowly stepped off the porch and quickly found myself with his gun in my hand. I vowed to destroy these creatures in the name of my father and God himself."

"And…have you? Were you able to find the creature that killed your father?"

"I did. About a week later just outside of Cheyenne. I thought it was over, but it had only just begun. I followed news across the state of similar creatures seen lurking in the darkened corners of towns or roaming the plains."

"You think one of those creatures is here? But, if that's true, why do we meet at night?"

He kissed her forehead and spoke gently. "You have nothing to fear, beautiful Annabelle. You are protected by God's light. And, should He somehow slip, you are protected by my father's pistol and my watchful eye."

Annabelle awoke as a sharp rock dug its way into her lower back. She was being dragged, but to where she couldn't make out. Her eyes struggled for clarity that refused to come.

"Get her in there, boys." Panic ravaged her thoughts as the kicked up dust from being dragged through the streets attacked her nostrils. Stones stuck their sharp points into her back and hips and she could feel her flesh beginning to tear. "There. In there. Close the doors," the voice hurriedly whispered.

The sudden drop of her legs startled her back to full consciousness. Annabelle looked around and could see she was in a stable. The smell of horse, hay, and shit attacked her nose aggressively. To her side were the three men huddled together, talking softly. She couldn't make out what they were saying, but two of the men looked far more riled up than the other.

"Enough, Earl. You can either have your share or get out. I don't fuckin' care either way at this point," the drunk man slurred amid his reddened face.

The man Annabelle assumed was Earl froze in place as the other two men made their way over to where she lie, bruised and sore.

"Oh, looky here, Bill. She's awake." The drunk man leaned in close. His putrid breath made the bile in her stomach rise into her throat. "I told you it would have been better for you to stay asleep, sweetheart. I guess you like pain." The drunk man ran his tongue over her forehead slowly, leaving a glistening trail of sticky mucus stinking on her brow. "She likes pain, Bill. Let's oblige the young lady."

Annabelle rolled slowly onto her stomach and tried to crawl away from the men as they laughed and kicked her legs. Her eyes were clear, but her speech was still garbled, and she discovered she was irritated with herself for being caught in such a position.

Maybe her love had seen her and was on his way. The thought kept her crawling forward, closer to the stable door yet still agonizingly far away.

"Alright, Bill. Enough with the games. I'm getting tired. I need a bit of release before bed. What about you, Earl? Last chance." The drunk said over his shoulder.

Annabelle kept crawling.

She couldn't see Earl's contemplative look, but Annabelle sensed him as he closed in on her. When Earl's large hands closed around her arms and turned her on her back, she finally screamed.

"No, no, get off of me, you animals! My man is waiting for me! He's coming."

The drunk man straddled her stomach and slapped her hard across the mouth.

"Oh, yeah, I'm sure he's going to bust through those doors any minute now." The drunk continued to laugh as he tore her dress off her shoulders and halfway down her body. Her exposed breasts riled the men up even more.

"Stop. Please, stop."

"Oh, we'll stop, young lady. But we need to get this poison out of us first."

Annabelle weakly punched against the drunk's chest, a desperate attempt to fight off the animal on top of her. The drunk laughed harder with every strike. Suddenly, he spat in her face. A small, chewed chunk of steak that hadn't been left in the street landed on Annabelle's lip. She turned her face and wept.

"Please…stop. I don't want anything bad to happen…"

"Unfortunately, young lady, we're past that point. Bill, Earl, hold her arms."

Bill immediately dove for her thrashing right hand. Earl hesitated, but eventually even he did as he was bade and held down her left arm.

"Ah, much better," the drunk said. "It'll feel better if you just give in to it, sweetheart." He tore her dress down further, exposing her innocence. He unbuckled his belt and pulled his pants down just far enough to pull himself out.

"Please…I don't want to hurt you," Annabelle pleaded.

Her words froze the men. They looked at each other with bewilderment.

"Her mind is gone. She's broken," Bill chuckled.

The drunk on top of Annabelle looked bothered for only a moment before he returned his focus to the ugly task he had set out to complete.

"This won't take long," the drunk slurred. "I like it when they buck like a bronco."

As he positioned himself at the right angle,

Annabelle struggled, squirmed, grunted, and groaned. Her muscles strained against the men holding her down and the animal about to violate her. Her face flushed, and she closed her eyes against the pain that began to rip her skin apart.

"Nooooo," she roared in a voice from another place. A darker place.

When the blood spatter splashed across the drunk's face, he was initially too stunned to move. When Bill's scream tore at his ears, he scrambled back on his hands in a crab-like manner. Earl howled and fell back when he noticed Bill's arm ripped from his shoulder and held in Annabelle's white-knuckled fist.

The Annabelle creature rose from her supine position, the bloody stump of Bill's arm dripping fat globs of red liquid on her feet. The beautiful young woman who had been dragged into the stable was transformed into a giant hideous creature of nightmares. The rest of her dress tore at the sudden immensity that tried to fit within it and fell to the ground.

Bill sat where he had been holding Annabelle down and screamed as he watched his lifeblood spurt out from the torn flesh of his shoulder. The Annabelle creature took two steps toward him, leaned down, and clubbed Bill's head with his own arm until it caved in on itself, a bloody crescent moon under the white moonlight sneaking between the beams of the stable.

The creature dropped the arm on Bill's lifeless body and turned suddenly on the drunk who had caused this. She stalked closer to him as he backpedaled, never taking his eyes off the blood-stained face of his would-be victim. His breath came in rapid, shallow gasps as his back pressed against the stable door. The creature stood just before him and leaned low, her warm breath drying the sweat on his brow.

"I like pain, remember? Let me show you."

She reached her inhuman hand around the drunk's throat and lifted him high off the ground. The drunk's feet kicked back and forth, not quite spanning the distance between himself and the creature. He tried to suck in breath but failed. His eyes became clouded and began to close.

When the creature's other hand went low, grabbed hold of his manhood, and tore, the drunk's eyes snapped open and tears flowed down his cheeks. The creature could feel his vocal cords straining to cry out, but the creature simply held tighter. She brought his penis close to her face and stared at it for only a moment before raising it above her head, squeezing the remaining blood out of it and into her mouth. Her cracked, gray tongue lapped at the blood; she licked her lips to clean up the spatters that hadn't gone directly down her throat. She then took the flaccid hunk of meat and slammed it into the drunk's gaping mouth so hard his head smashed right through the stable door.

She let his soft body fall to the ground and grunted a self-satisfied noise. She was about to sit down and relax in the corner, desperate to get to her love, when she heard a soft sob behind her.

The creature turned and saw Earl in the corner, his weak legs somehow keeping him upright. The front of his jeans had turned a dark blue, and there was a stench of shit that the Annabelle creature was sure wasn't from the unraked manure. The creature sneered and took a long stride toward him.

"No. No, please. I didn't want this to happen. I tried to talk them out of it. They…they wouldn't listen."

The creature closed the distance in only a few short strides and stood before the shaking man. She let her hair fall over her eyes and lowered her brow. She got so close that her blood-stained breasts pressed against the man's shirt, leaving two dark red circles to match the dark blue stain on his pants. She placed her hands on both sides of his head and raised it slowly. The Annabelle creature flicked the hair back from her eyes and stared deep into Earl's.

"Oh my God," Earl sputtered out just before Annabelle gave one quick twist of his head, turning it completely around. Earl collapsed at her feet.

The Annabelle creature put her hands on her knees and bent forward, sucking breath in slowly and lowering its heart rate. The soft night breeze slipped through the cracks in the walls, purifying the metallic smell of blood in the stable. Her body slowly started to return to its normal size. But, then her heart skipped when she heard a voice she didn't expect.

"I've finally found you, creature."

The voice she'd recognize anywhere. The voice she'd be able to identify throughout time.

She turned slowly and saw her love in the open doorway, his father's pistol pointed at her chest. Annabelle's face had begun to return to normal, and she pleaded to him with eyes that begged understanding.

"My love, please…"

"You can't fool me, demon. Back to hell where you belong."

The bullet was out of the pistol and into her heart

before she could say another word. Annabelle stood momentarily, dead without acknowledgment, before falling to the ground and fully transforming back to her human form.

The man walked over to her motionless body and knelt down. He took her head in his arms and bent low, kissing her forehead.

"I loved a lie," he said quietly. "May you burn with the rest of them."

The man rose, lightly placing Annabelle's head on the ground. He turned and walked out of the stable, the bright white light of the moon guiding his path out of town.

2. Earth Stood Hard As Iron, Water Like A Stone
DE McCluskey (1900 – 1920's)

Note from the author:

Unlike you Yankee colonists and bloody usurpers, my story is written in the King's own script…

While it may look to you chaps as if some things are out of place, or the occasional letter U has been added, please be aware that the colourful euphemisms we use in our neighbourhood are the correct ones… and if I wasn't far too busy drinking my English breakfast tea, snacking on cheese, and delighting in full flavoured scones with fresh cream and strawberry jam… I would bloody well be over there with my red pen and my t-shirt stating that we won two bloody wars before you bothered your arses to turn up… and setting the records straight.

A good day to you…

DE McCluskey

1.

The ground was white. It was as pale as bones from a body that had been stripped of all flesh. The ride had been an awful experience, one that had almost shaken the poor professor to his own bones. The carriage wheels felt as if they had hit every single pothole in the road, perhaps even swerving across the carriageway ensuring said wheels hit the few the horses missed.

The professor had hit the roof of the carriage a number of times to warn the driver he was still there, he was still alive, and he was most displeased with the beating he'd endured.

The cold had been insatiable. It had been like this for a few weeks now. A relentless, gnawing cold that had a way of seeping through the very fabric of the clothes one was wearing, no matter how many layers had been laid, to consume whatever scant warmth the flesh beneath them might have been harbouring.

Professor John Harding of Oxford University had stepped off the carriage feeling like a man a full twenty years older than the fifty-one he'd endured on this planet. The last twenty coming in the last hour of the journey from Oxford to London in this deep mid-winter. This was a time where he enjoyed nothing more than the comforts his tenure at the university offered him and his good lady wife. She had refused this invitation, but it had been made perfectly clear to the good Professor that this presentation would be well worth his efforts.

He didn't believe the boast for one moment, but the time he had spent couped up with Mrs. Harding in the university had been long and laborious, and although he loved his wife deeply, he savoured the chance to be apart from her for one night. It was promised to be a night of brandy, cigars, deep and meaningful conversation with peers, and of course, a collection of new and fine winter art.

He begrudgingly paid the cab driver handsomely. The poor fellow deserved a little something extra for sitting up there in this weather for that journey, even if he had steered the horses into every hole.

'Don't forget, I'll need to be collected at one, prompt, tomorrow afternoon. Be on time, and there will be more where that came from, my good man,' he informed the driver as the man counted the coins he had handed him.

A smile broke on his ruddy face. 'I won't let you down, sir,' he replied enthusiastically. 'Enjoy your presentation.'

'I'm sure I will, my buck. Now be off with you

before this cold eats into your bones.'

'Aw, I'm sure I'm hardier than I appear, Professor. The horses however…'

Harding laughed at this before waving the man and his fine steeds off into the snowy grounds of Lighthouse Manor, which sat on the outskirts of Fulham, a leafy and prosperous area of Greater London.

'Harding, you made it,' the booming voice of one of his oldest friends cut through the whistling of the wind.

Harding looked up to see the portly, robust figure of Mark Cranston standing in the doorway of the mansion, twelve stone steps above him.

'Thank the Lord,' Cranston continued. 'I was beginning to think you were going to leave me here with this boring rabble.'

Harding looked up and grinned at his welcome committee. 'Not on your life, my good friend. You know I've been looking forward to this for months.'

'Come into the warmth, man. I have a fine V.S.O.P with your name written all over it.'

Before he knew anything else, a servant had relieved him of his bags, and he had been whisked into the warmth of the very grand Lighthouse Manor. A large glass had been thrust into his hands, and a thick cigar had been all but forced into his mouth and lit. His coat had been taken, as had his boots, replaced with the most comfortable carpet slippers his feet had ever had the fortune of caressing.

'Come now, old man. We're almost ready to begin,' Cranston boomed as he slapped Harding on the back, almost hard enough for him to drop his brandy. 'Remind me to show you the private collection at the end of the presentation,' he whispered, leaning conspiratorially into Harding's ear. 'They are a little… risqué, should we say. For the discerning gentleman, eh?' He grinned and winked before letting Harding go and storming off into the ballroom. Harding was left in the hallway, shaking his head and chuffing to himself. He drew in a deep breath and took a drag from the excellent cigar he was holding.

Cranston was a patron of the erotic, as was the good Lady Cranston, and Harding had braced himself for more of the unusual nudes of his wife, cavorting with the staff, many of which Harding had noticed were of the negro persuasion.

They were the ones she seemed to prefer her dalliances with.

He took another swig of the brandy and followed his host into the ballroom.

2.

The whole presentation had been a rather boorish affair. There was a new artist on the scene who had taken Cranston's eye, and he had decided to play philanthropist and help the youth on his journey. The talk had been amusing enough, and the artwork had been somewhat provoking. Some of it was visibly stunning, captivating, and in a few cases, breathtaking.

Harding had little interest in the artwork itself; he was here for the social aspect of the event, and he had revelled in it, perhaps a little too much.

The V.S.O.P. brandy was, as usual, excellent, and he had partaken in more than a few large glasses, a good few more than perhaps he should have. *Why not?* he thought to himself with a chuckle. *Am I not worth a few dalliances? Not in the same way as Lady Cranston,* he continued with another chuckle. His amusement continued as he saw the Lady of the manor, obviously drunk, even more than he was, talking and fawning over a short fat man Harding recognised as a doctor of some note, although he couldn't remember his name. The short man couldn't help but fawn over the Lady's shapely figure, no doubt replaying the pictures Cranston enjoyed presenting in his drunken head.

'My man,' Cranston interrupted his amusement.

'Come and meet our artist. I think you will find him a perfect court jester.' Harding nodded as he removed himself from the blissful warmth of the roaring fire in the hearth. He felt his hand being tugged with some force, pulling him over to the other side of the room.

The youth he found himself thrust before was an unsettling type. His hair was far too long. It was almost in a style that would suit his wife, not one that was suitable for a gentleman, unless he was from a godforsaken, liberal European country. His clothes hung from his body as if they were not his, and there was a… grubbiness to him. Harding didn't like the term but was at a loss for any other way to describe the man he was being introduced to.

'Professor Harding, this is Louis Van Halte. Don't worry, he's not one of those boorish Norwegians. He's from right here in the city. I found him on a street corner. Can you believe that? A boy of such talent, plying his trade to the beggars and unfortunates. My wife instantly fell in love with him, and his work…'

I bet she did, Harding thought, hiding a smile.

'… so, I snapped him up and set him up with a studio, right here in the manor.'

'Your servant, sir,' Harding said, holding his hand out to the youth.

Cranston shook his head. 'Oh, the boy doesn't speak. He won't shake your hand either. He's a true artist, eccentric and a magician, as I'm sure you have found out for yourself.'

'Oh, yes. I have to say I am enthralled by your work,' Harding gushed.

The boy looked at him, nodded, and then walked away towards a door over the other side of the room.

'A real conversationalist, eh?'

Cranston laughed. 'His art does all the talking for him.'

'So, what is the work you wanted to show me privately?' Harding added. Lady Cranston was a beautiful woman, and he did rather enjoy the photographs, and the oiled paintings of her. 'I'm eager to see what this youth's eye has brought forth that you see fit to have a private audience.'

'Oh, these pieces are exquisite,' Cranston gushed.

'They will have you all frozen in awe!'

'I bet they will.'

'I must dash. I need to make sure that the good

Lady Cranston is engaged. These pieces are not for delicate eyes, like hers.'

Harding was intrigued now. 'Are they different from what you normally show us?' he whispered, making sure no one was in earshot of the question.

Cranston looked over towards his wife. He licked his lips and swallowed. The action, although small, was rather quite telling. Harding got the feeling that the new pieces might not have anything to do with the Lady this time.

Disappointment wracked him. 'Oh, these pieces are true art, my dear man. They are like nothing you will have ever seen before in your life.'

'What makes them so different?'

'They are truly works of…'

Cranston paused, as if for dramatic effect. All this did was annoy Harding. 'Works of what, man?'

'You will see.'

As Cranston moved to take his leave, Harding reached out and grabbed his arm. 'Thomas. Works of what?'

Cranston allowed himself to pull back and looked Harding straight in the eyes. Harding fancied he could see something in his host's eyes. Something skirting on the edge of sanity. Cranston looked around the room at the drunken revellers, with his eyes finally resting on his wife. A ghost of a smile broke on his features.

Harding didn't care for that smile at all.

'Grotesquerie,' he whispered.

Harding's brow creased. 'What?'

Cranston's eyes glared momentarily. The thrill of the word he had just uttered filled them with a sick illumination. 'You heard me, old man. The boy has promised us a live performance. He is going to actively create a work of art, right before our eyes. He has called it, *'The Earth Stood Hard As Iron, Water Like A Stone.'*

Harding tried to hide his revulsion of the misapplication of the title. It sounded to him like a perversion of the popular, gentle Christmas Carol. It didn't sound like something that should be used as a title of a... *what did he call it? Grotesquerie.*

Before he could question him again, Cranston had shaken off Harding's hold and was away, thrusting himself back into the thinning crowd within the manor. Harding watched him passing through the men, talking, whispering, laughing, and cajoling. He noticed that most of his host's attention was focused on his lady wife, who was doing much the same as he was.

He drained his glass of brandy and looked around

for a servant who would be able to procure another for him, but it seemed there were none about, so he decided to go on a quest to refill it himself. For some reason he thought a belly full of brandy might be needed for what he was about to be subjected to in the after hours of this party.

The decanter in the hall was empty, so he made his way out, heading towards the area of the kitchens that he knew were along the short but darkened corridor. He was roughly halfway towards his destination when he heard the door to the ballroom open, and a shaft of light briefly illuminated him.

He thought nothing of it at first, until he heard the whispers. One was female, of this he was quite certain. The other, well the other was nothing short of a mumbling. Even though he couldn't quite make out what the woman was saying, he had an inkling the male voice was either talking gibberish, or some kind of foreign language he was not frequented with. Hastings was conversant in French, and German, and also had a grasp of Latin, but this was something different. It was a tongue he was not only unfamiliar with, but one that unnerved him. He felt along the wall until he found a small nook that was large enough for him to slip inside. Something in his instincts told him he should not be discovered by this couple in whatever adventure they were endeavouring.

The shaft of light dissipated as the door to the ballroom closed with a muffled bang. The brief light had stolen all his ability to see correctly in the gloom. Therefore, when the odd couple ushered past him, he could not see who they were. Although he did have an idea it might have been Lady Cranston, he was basing this assumption on the smell of her perfume. He could have been wrong, but by the way she was giggling as they passed, he didn't think he was.

Harding shook his head.

He was by no means a prude. He'd had his fair share of concubines in his day, and he had admitted to himself that the photographs of Lady Cranston with the coloureds in her employment had aroused him fully. However, he didn't completely agree with the wanton hedonism the Cranstons employed in the course of their marriage.

Within a moment they were passed, and he was able to continue his own adventure. *The Quest for Cognac.* He giggled at this thought, but had to stifle his laugh as it sounded, to him, at least five times louder than he had meant it, especially in the erstwhile silence of the corridor.

Within five minutes he was back in the ballroom, his glass fuller than it had been before he had left.

In direct comparison, the ballroom was a lot emptier than when he had left it.

There were very few people left. Of the ones who remained, all of them were men, and most he knew, either personally, or by reputation. They were all men of business. Some of them were Lords, like Cranston. It would have been considered *good company* if Harding didn't know what they were here for.

'Gentlemen, can I please have your attention?'

Harding looked around to see Cranston standing at the head of the room. The smart dinner jacket he'd adorned all evening had been removed and replaced with a rather thick overcoat. The collars were pulled up tight around his head, and he was holding a pair of thick leather gloves in his hands.

All the mumbling and drunken conversations ceased as everyone turned to regard their host.

Harding looked at the faces of his fellow revellers, he could read the eagerness in their eyes. They were all, without exception, expecting more of the same lurid and graphic photographs of the delectable Lady, in flagrante, as they called it in smarter circles.

'As you are all gentlemen of fine repute and have all

been known to enjoy a taste of the erotic, and the exotic, I have something very special to share with you this year. So, pray you all don your overcoats, and your hats, as we are about to venture into the grounds.'

This announcement was the cause of consternation among the invited, but as they had never once been let down by Cranston before, they all agreed to retrieve their outdoor wear from the butler in the cloakroom.

'What in the fresh hell is going on?' an older man asked Harding as he wrapped himself in a long, woollen overcoat. Harding recognised the man as a judge, and a rather important one at that.

'I have no idea,' he slurred. The extra-large glass of brandy he had helped himself to was taking its effect on him. 'But knowing old Cranston, I have no doubt it will be something spectacular.'

He had no idea why he'd said this to the old man, as he wasn't really looking forward to whatever the Grotesquerie might turn out to be. He retrieved his own coat and buttoned it up to the very top button. He fixed his thick scarf, and slipped his hands deep into the sheepskin gloves his wife had given him as a Christmas present. He then picked up his brandy glass with both hands, as his fingers were far too encumbered to allow him to pick it up correctly. He put it to his mouth and drained it to the very last drop. After placing the glass back down on the mahogany sideboard, he followed the gathering towards the French windows that framed the games room, leading onto the large patio, and the grounds, that included a large lake beyond.

The wind hit him the instant he stepped out of the shelter of the house. The brandy currently sloshing around in his stomach did nothing to stave him from the cold of that dark, January night. It tore at his coat, which was still damp from the journey in the carriage. Wherever it could, its icy fingers pierced the woollen fabric and poked hungrily at the flesh beneath it. He fancied he could feel unholy talons tearing at him. His face, the only part of his body not sheltered from the wind, was instantly ravaged. His eyes watered as the wind hit them, drying them momentarily. Then the instant flurries of freezing rain, or maybe it was sleet, hit his cheeks, stinging them, making them redder than they had ever been. If it hadn't been for the relative warmth created by the twelve or thirteen other men who were stepping and shuffling around him, he might have called it a day, and retired back to the house for another brandy, one last cigar, and then his bed. The gathered colleagues buoyed each other on, enthused by the antics of Lady Cranston, and whatever it was she was up to now. They chattered incessantly, mostly, Hastings thought, to forget how utterly desolate it was out here in the elements.

'A man could get frostbite in five minutes out here,' he heard one man mutter.

He was inclined to agree with this assessment.

'Gentlemen, thank you for assembling here in the grounds of this manor on this most inclement of nights. I can assure you this presentation will be brief, and it will be complete. We had to take it out in this climate in order to produce the level, and the quality work my protégé here, Mr Louis Van Halte had promised us. Please indulge me, my friends. There is somewhat of a backstory to this event. It is one, where if you will indulge me once again, I will regale you with presently.'

The mumbling between the gathered men voiced their impatience to escape the freezing weather and get back into the embrace of the warmth of the mansion, not to mention the embrace of the flowing selections of brandies and whiskey on offer.

Harding was intrigued, possibly more than the others since he had been informed of the Grotesquerie, and had been guessing what it could have been ever since. He glanced around at the gathering and noticed the absence of two prominent members. Lady Cranston and Van Halte himself. They were nowhere to be seen. In fact, he hadn't seen them since his adventure to the kitchens earlier.

'Please, my good friends, and scholars, cast your great minds back ten winters since. The great freeze of 1891 to be precise.'

There were a number of murmurs through the crowd. Everyone remembered that winter. The ground had started to freeze from the middle of November, and it hadn't relented its hold until long into February. The worst of it happened over the Christmas period, and well into January. People called it Biblical. It was a cold grim reaper that reaped so many souls that year, as the temperatures plummeted. The record low was recorded as lower than minus ten, perhaps double that, and it stayed in that state for weeks on end.

'Does anyone remember the artist who emerged from that great winter?' Cranston asked.

Again, there were nods among the men, although not all of them were agreeable.

A macabre artisan had emerged in the city of London. His life-like structures of peasants, and unfortunates, caught in the throes of despair had caused quite the stir among the community. They were offered for display in the more fashionable boutiques of the city, and people called from miles around, some as far as Scotland, to see them, and marvel at their grotesque realism.

The artist was taken into the embrace of the city, and he managed to infuse the structures into the very hearts of the nation, at a time when the population were dying of hypothermia, and other complications of the cold, in their droves.

The popularity waned greatly when the thaw began in February, and the artist disappeared from the face of the earth, some say overnight. The statues, the marbled grotesques that had been the symbolisation of the mighty freeze began to melt. When they did, it became clear that they were not statues. They had not been carved from marble, or even from ice as some had claimed.

They were the frozen corpses of the thousands of unfortunates who had passed due to the extreme cold. He had sold the great city of London its very own shame, and the people had bought it.

The artist fled, and was never to be seen, or even heard of, again.

'Well tonight, for your pleasure, I, Lord Cranston,

have a monumental surprise for you. Normally, I would now be delighting you with blown up photographs of my dear wife's indiscretions with the staff, especially those men of colour.'

Again, there were murmurs around the crowd. Harding was still searching among the faces for any sign of the artist, or of Lady Cranston. He marvelled at the cloud of mist hanging over the cold throng of semi-drunken men. Some of them were slapping each other on the backs at the mention of Lady Cranston, and there were more than one or two salacious jeers.

'Well, tonight, my fine fellows, my surprise for you is a tribute to that very artist who was so celebrated in our city, before fleeing as a fugitive. My ward, Mr Van Halte has been studying these works, and has produced, for our viewing pleasure, a casting in tribute to the poor unfortunates who were taken from our city and posed for all and sundry to gawp at. This work, he has not even allowed me to see.'

The group fell silent as two men, servants in the employ of Cranston, wheeled a large cart out from somewhere in the darkness of the garden. Steam was rising from the tops of their heads as they laboured with their cargo, giving the illusion that the men could very well be on fire. The throng around

Harding remained still silent, although a great many of them, Harding included, were hopping from foot to foot in a vain attempt to keep warm. Everyone's interest heaped upon the veiled work mounted on the carriage.

Cranston was beaming almost from ear to ear as he shared his gaze between these newcomers and the members of the crowd gathered in his grounds. He made his way over to his men who were labouring with whatever was beneath the thin tarpaulin.

'Where is he?' he rasped to the two men.

Both looked at their master and shrugged.

Harding stepped forwards, breaking from the crowd. 'Are you looking for this Van Halte chap?' he asked.

Cranston turned from his men and looked at Harding. The look on his face was a mixture of wild beast and confused old man. 'Who else would I be looking for?' he hissed.

Harding stepped back, as if slapped. 'My friend, all I wanted to tell you was that I saw Van Halte, along with your lady wife, not an hour ago. They were heading for the games room, or maybe beyond.'

'The games room you say?' Cranston asked, his wide eyes narrowing on him.

Harding nodded.

'Excellent,' he said as if in reply, but in all honesty it sounded to Harding, as if he were talking to himself. 'Then he must have finished his work. No matter where the blighter is now, all that matters is that he has finished his tribute.'

'Tribute?' Harding asked.

'Yes. His tribute to the great sculptor who disappeared some ten years ago.'

'Sir, you can't tell me that you will be paying tributes to a demented mass murderer. That is not right. It flays in the face of God himself.'

'Ah, but do you not see my good man? The artist in question was highlighting the sin, the very debauchery of a disgustingly vile city lost to Sodom.'

'I don't get you. What is it you are saying?'

'The artist was not killing his subjects. He was only highlighting the sin that the poor unfortunates of the city lived and died for.'

Harding didn't like where this was going. He was shaking his head as he raised his hand in the air, getting the attention of Cranston. 'But, sir. You yourself live an alternative lifestyle. You allow your wi… Lady Cranston, her liberties. You record them for your own pleasure. You allow us to…'

The grin on Cranston's face was complete. Any glimpses of sanity Harding thought he might have seen earlier were gone. Complete and utter madness had taken over him. It blazed out from his eyes. Harding fancied he could smell it on him, on his breath and on his sweat, even through the freezing temperatures.

'My dear friends. Allow me to unveil my commissioned tribute,' he shouted to the gathered men. 'However, I have just one condition you must adhere to before I reveal, for your delight, the Grotesquery.'

The men, including Harding who had gone back to his place in the small crowd, all looked at each other. A group of maybe ten servants appeared out of the darkness around them. All of them were armed with pistols, one or two of them had rifles in their possession. Each of the weapons were raised and pointed into the small crowd.

'I'm afraid I'll need each of you to disrobe.'

This caused a loud murmur of consternation.

'Disrobe? Are you mad, man?' Harding shouted above the hubbub. 'It's ten below out here, possibly less. There is no way any of us are going to…'

There was a loud crack. It was followed by the smell of cordite in the frigid air, and the falling of someone within the crowd. Harding knew the man; he was a doctor of some repute in the city. He fell to the ground, blood spurting from the recent wound in his head. As it spurted, it spattered over a few of the others, causing a panic within them. Everyone pushed in an attempt to get away from the dead doctor and keep their distance from the armed servants around them. The servants, including the one with the still smoking rifle, took a step closer.

'My friends, I can not allow you to leave, not just yet. All I ask is one simple thing. You all must disrobe. I do not understand your hesitancy. You have all been privy to the Lady Cranston's nakedness, and her debauched ways. All I ask is you return the favour to her. She requests to see you all disrobed, and naked, and as you know whatever Lady Cranston wants, Lady Cranston gets.'

Without further preamble, he pulled on the tarpaulin that covered the work on the waggon.

Everyone, without exception, other than the dead doctor who everyone had now seemed to have forgotten in their haste to escape this situation, gasped.

'Isn't this what you want, my dear?' Cranston asked as he looked away from the men gathered in a small, tight circle.

Beneath the tarpaulin was *the* most grotesque thing Harding had ever seen in his life. It was Lady

Cranston. Yes, she was naked, but she was quite dead. She was frozen. That on its own was not the only grotesque image. Before, and behind her, were two of Cranston's men. They were the coloured servants we had seen the Lady cavorting with before. One of them, the man before her, was standing rather proud. His genitalia was in an aroused state and was deep with her mouth. The second, standing behind her, had also entered the woman.

All three were dead.

They were the tributes to the artist's work, ten years prior.

'Van Halte,' Harding gasped, tearing his eyes from the frozen depravity before him.

'Gentlemen, I will not ask again. I now demand that you disrobe at once, otherwise poor old Doctor Huberg will not be the only one lying dead from a bullet on my lawn.'

There was glee in his voice. Harding could hear it. It sickened him, but more than that, it petrified him.

'DISROBE… AT ONCE!' Cranston bellowed.

The armed servants took another step closer.

Harding began removing his gloves, followed by his overcoat. It wasn't long before the others joined in their de-clothing.

'All of it,' Cranston shouted. 'My wife wants to see you in all of your glory.' He was laughing as he shouted, his wide eyes scanning all of the shedding men on his lawn.

It didn't take long before all of them were nude, and shivering.

There were nine men standing on the grass, all of them quivering, all of them trying their very best to cover their near frozen modesty. All of them with guns pointed at them.

Heaps of clothing were scattered upon the ground around them.

'Don't you think this is only fair? All of you have revelled in the sins of my wife. You were all happy to laugh along with me as I existed in constant torment, in a pure embarrassment. Didn't any of you think about me living as the laughing stock of the whole city? That dirty slut, who I called my wife, cavorting with the staff, and the coloureds, and all of you enjoying my humiliation. Revelling in my shame.'

'Come now man,' Harding stuttered, as he stepped gingerly forward, his hand covering his shrunken privates. 'N…n…no one was l…l…laughing at you. We w…w…ere j… jealous of you, that your w…wife…' as he stuttered this word, his eyes flicked to the vile ornament on the wagon. 'Was living a life that was f…f…free. We all ass…umed you revelled with her too.'

'Did you now? Did you ever think to ask me? While you so called friends, were out fucking your wives, or your mistresses, or your cousins, did you ever once spare a thought for me, alone in my chambers while my wife was doing…' He pointed at the effigy. '…this?'

Someone else stepped out of the darkness around them.

All their heads turned to witness the small figure of Van Halte emerging from the shadows. He was holding something in his hands, dragging it behind him. It looked like some kind of tube.

Cranston looked at the youth. 'Ah, there you are my fine fellow. Did you find what you needed?'

The boy held up the tube for Cranston to see. All the others looked too.

It was a pipe. A very long one. It looked to be made of linen, as it trailed off into the darkness in the direction of the house.

'This tube, my fine men, is connected to a faucet in the house, and one of my loyal servants is in the process of turning that faucet on. The water that will travel through the linen will be very cold. Very cold indeed.'

Harding looked towards the youth holding the pipe. It was then he noticed the youth wasn't young at all. He was a lot older than he had initially thought. He was a man, one with a crazed expression encompassing his face.

'Yes. I'm sorry to inform you of my error, earlier. You see, this effigy before me, the one of my whore wife being serviced, is *not* a tribute. It is part one of a comeback of sorts. Van Halte here is a true artist, and like any real artist, his art *has* to be made. So, you see, Lady Cranston was the first in a new series. This one is called Earth Stood Hard As Iron, Water Like A Stone. You gentlemen are to be the centrepiece of this work.'

With that, as if on cue, ice-cold water streamed from the end of the pipe Van Halte was holding.

The water cascaded over the shivering, naked men. They all began to scream as the freezing water fell over them.

Harding tried his very best to shelter behind another man but was not allowed any succour. He watched through tear-filled eyes as Van Halte, and Cranston, danced merrily around the throng of soaking, freezing men. Van Halte continued spraying, taking great lengths to make sure he thoroughly soaked *all* of them.

The frigid air was so cold that the water had the effect of hundreds of thousands of tiny, iced daggers, cutting into the pale, freezing flesh of the best London society had to offer.

Some of it froze in the air and was very near a frozen sludge as it coated their bodies.

Harding, screaming at the agony, and the indignation of this scene, rallied a few of the others and attempted to charge the armed men surrounding them, but sharp agony-inducing whacks to their faces caused them to drop to their knees as the butts of the rifles broke their noses.

Begrudgingly, they all began to lie on the soggy ground, shivering in the freezing mud. The men were no longer caring about their nakedness, as the icy sludge spraying from the pipe covered them, creating a vile quagmire beneath them.

The mud hardened rapidly in the frigid air.

As it did, Harding could feel his racing heart begin to slow.

A strange warmth snaked through him as his shaking limbs began to slow too.

As the comforting blanket of darkness enveloped him, his head was filled with the moans and cries of his fellow exhibitions, along with his own.

3.

An odd exhibition was discovered in the centre of the city the very next morning. It was displayed in a rather prominent location, one that was chosen to maximise its visibility.

The display was that of a naked lady being sexually serviced by two men, while ten others stood around watching the proceedings. It was difficult to tell if the men were laughing, or if they were screaming. The only thing anyone could really tell for certain, was that these thirteen people were quite dead.

One of them had a bullet wound to his head.

A plaque with the words THE EARTH STOOD HARD AS IRON, WATER LIKE A STONE – A DEDICATION TO MY WHORE WIFE had been hammered into the frozen ground before the gruesome sculpture.

On further investigation it was found that the likeness of the woman resembled that of Lady Angela Cranston. This shocked the populous, but not as much as the shock of discovering the ten men, the ones standing around, nakedly enjoying the cavorting, were all prominent men of the city; Professors, reverends, doctors, and politicians, alike.

The police set out a warrant for Cranston. They knew he had been hosting a lavish party at his manor the night before, and the higher echelon of the police had been invited.

Their investigations concluded at Lighthouse Manor.

A single gunshot had travelled through his chin, before continuing into his brain. It had sprayed the contents of his head all over the wall behind the desk he had been sitting at. A note was found in his handwriting, stating he would no longer be the laughing stock of society. It further stated that art had been his preferred method of vengeance.

Of Van Halte, there was no sign. The similarities between the gruesome display, and the ones that had plagued the city ten years prior, were not lost on the police, yet no matter how hard they looked for the man, he eluded their search.

The artist had slipped away into the darkness of the winter, once again, taking his twisted methods with him.

3. Bottles and Bruises
Laura Bilodeau (1920 – 1940's)

"Men are nicotine soaked, beer besmirched, whiskey greased, red eyed devils." Well… at least that's what our idol, Carrie A. Nation has to say. And we agree, but that's just to put it lightly. Our husbands, fathers, sons, brothers, neighbors, friends, all of the male sect have all become drunkards. They've turned their souls from their families, and have found solitude at the bottoms of bottles; locked away beneath banks and shops in towns. Their livelihoods reside within their liquors. Their actions traitorous, their ways, blasphemous, we will have no more. We will stand up at once, against our society of men, and take back what's ours. For life, for love, for liberty. For we are the Tiverton Titty Toting Temperance Totality, 5T for short. We will do what must be done, at all costs, we are the girl's girls.

Just another Monday morning at the beauty salon,

and Millicent arrived donning new blacks and blues all over her. Don't get it confused though, she wasn't wearing makeup. These are bruises left as a reminder of Archie's late night at the speakeasy last night. Her discolorations have been a common occurrence for the past few months, becoming more and more frequent as of late. But, she's not the only woman adorned with them. Many a woman have come in, too battered and disheveled to press their faces with powders, and their rouge being too dark to discern from the beatings. Millicent looked sheepishly around the room filled similarly with all women, all of which are friends, and cleared her throat.

"Listen up! Haven't you all heard of Carrie Nation?"

"No Millie, who is she?" asked Connie quizzically, her hair sitting atop her head in tight rollers.

"Well ladies, listen closely, because she is the answer to many of our, and the rest of society's problems. She was a radical prohibitionist who many people called 'Hatchet Granny.' She stormed saloons, depleting their stashes of beer and liquor by way of rocks and eventually the use of a hatchet. She was arrested countless times, but never faltered in her beliefs that alcohol was the downfall of our society and turned our men into monsters."

The women in the salon gasped realizing what Millie was onto.

"What are you implying, Millie?"

"We are going to stop these motherfuckers in their tracks. They won't lay a hand on any one of us, or a bottle ever again. Are you with me?"

An instant thunderous cheer roared through the walls of the small salon. The women were prancing around giddy with a newfound excitement and jubilance they didn't have before Millicent's comments. Millie didn't expect such an exuberant and resoundingly positive response from the others. The Great Depression caused precisely that among many Americans, a *great depression*, so this vibrant display before her was a very welcome sight for sore eyes.

"We leave tonight. Once these drunkards are off to 'do business' we know where they'll really be. There is no time to waste planning for days in advance and risk being caught, stopped or swayed. We'll stop them before they even have a chance to walk back through our front doors reeking of whiskey and stale cigarettes at the break of dawn. Go home, eat a plentiful meal, hydrate yourselves, rest your feet, and pray to your higher powers. Take what you can. Anything can be a weapon if you're clever and willing. Make sure to wear extra layers, protect yourselves at all costs. Do what must be done. Victory is ours, ladies. Now, let's go powder our noses and meet back here at dusk."

Millicent spoke with a confidence and pride the women had never seen,. There was a fire in her eyes that burned hot enough to spark that very same fire in all of the others. Her voice was loud and stable; it didn't tremble, not once. She stood straight, made eye contact, and never looked down her nose at anyone. Everyone was equal to Millie, except for the lousy bastards that called themselves men.

Hours passed, then one by one, slowly but surely, each of the women began reappearing back at Betty's Beauty Salon. The regulars called it BB's for short. Millicent, of course, was the first to show. She wore a long, pale-yellow dress, pleated and adorned with pastel flowers. Atop the dress she layered a similarly colored canvas apron, still smudged and smeared with batter of the cookies she was baking when her husband set off for a "meeting" just a short while ago. In the pockets of her apron she hid large rocks, just as Carrie had done. Many of the rocks she collected from around the well behind her home and within her garden, carefully selecting those which were jagged or the most dense. Beneath her apron she wore a wide belt where she concealed a ball peen hammer, a rolling pin, a large kitchen knife, a variety of thick sticks that she had whittled down to fine points, and a small bag of chocolate covered pretzels. That girl didn't go anywhere without a little snacky snack. She didn't get those voluptuous curves Archie once bragged about by gnawing on celery sticks, you know?

Connie and Maggie arrived next. They were neighbors, so naturally they did most everything together. The two women, though they didn't say much, were a force to be reckoned with. You could see them coming all the way down the road. They were as wide as they were tall, and they came by way of horse and buggy. This would be the means of transportation for the women on this glorious night. Their horses, Victory and Mailliw, were large and in charge. They walked in perfect unison and just exuded confidence with every step.

Several other women staggered in wielding weapons of all sorts. Ruth, the town baker, even showed up with an old musket that her dad left to her when he passed away the year before.

"Tonight, we take back what's ours. We leave our fears at this very door and take no regrets home with us. These men, these bar owners, and anyone who comes between us will pay. Sacrifices must be made. Some of us may not make it out in the same shape we went in, but for the sake of our futures, we know what must be done."

A cacophony of elated and agreeable cheers erupted around her as the women pumped their fists into the air.

The women piled into the carriages and made their relentless journey toward the first known speakeasy in town, of all places, beneath the town jail… talk about crooked cops. This speakeasy was believed to be the most popular. It was the closest to the outskirts of the downtown area which led into the part of town where most people lived. The hidden escape was in such close proximity to the police station and other town officials that immediately following shifts, any number of elected and appointed officers could be seen slipping through the concealed entryway.

Millie led the group towards the back entrance while Connie and Maggie tied up the horses along the side of the building. They whinnied as she rounded the corner back towards the group in an almost telling way of what was to come. Millie cocked her dominant arm back far behind her body, and with every ounce of anger and effort she could muster, she swung her hatchet into the empty whiskey barrels, cracking and shattering them into pieces in front of her. Blow after blow, she didn't stop swinging until the barrels were surmounted to a pile of woodchips on the ground and a measly few scraps of metal. Behind the barrels hid a stainless steel door that was painted over to match the color of the wall around it.

A rustling could be heard coming from behind the doorway along with a muddled mixture of various voices. The women raised their weapons defensively and held their anticipatory breaths even deeper than they had already been. Tensions were high, and the hair on the back of everyone's necks stood at attention like proper soldiers awaiting salute.

Lo and behold, who other than Archie popped his head out from the opening in the wall. Time stood still temporarily, and with zero hesitation, Millie leapt forward, striking Archie across the head between his eye socket and temporal lobe with the rolling pin. If you were watching from a fly on the wall's perspective, you would've summed the whole motion up as though she were some crime-fighting superhero in the next edition of the weekly comic strip. The force and angle she hit him with unexpectedly went beyond that of stunning the man. It completely blew out his orbital lobe, creating more of a meteor-looking void above his cheek than an eye. A geyser of blood spewed out instantly, but Millie just kept dealing out hit after hit. The man's eye released from the socket, plopping onto the ground before him with a squelching sound, still connected by its entrails of whatever connective tissue holds one's eye in place. Millicent stomped on that as well, grinding it under her foot into the earth beneath. A sickening, sludgy, mudpie of eyeball goop and dirt formed beneath her foot, causing a few of the women to gag audibly and back away. Archie instinctively threw his hands up to protect his face and remaining eye.

Archie's weak attempt at defense and pleas of peace were promptly met with the back of Connie's hand, who felt compelled to join in Millicent's relentless attack.

"You no good, heartless dirtbag. Is this what you call business? Drinking away our only savings? Carelessly leaving your wife home alone to tend to the crops and homestead? Spending countless hours here huddled up in some hideaway hut only to return home and paint my face black and blue with your own two hands? How dare you call yourself a husband, nevertheless a man. You disgust me!"

The remainder of the women had all now arrived by that point and joined in with chants and hollers in support of Millicent. The ruckus unsurprisingly stirred other husbands from the safety of their hiding places within the dwelling to assess the chaos.

"CURTIS? Are you serious? You told me you were out of town checking out a new horse for us to bring home!" Ruth shouted.

"R-Ruth… what are you doing here? Why aren't you home? What are you all doing here? What is this!" Curtis shouted, very clearly confused by the spectacle before him.

"You've been gone for three days! Where on earth have you stayed?"

Ruth must have grown tired of the delayed response because less than a moment later, what once was an Adam's apple in Curtis' throat became a gaping and steaming hole. She lifted the musket without a tremble and blew a single pellet right through the center of his esophagus with such precision even a sharpshooter would have had to aim twice.

The following moments were cloaked in a silence that hung heavily in the air. The only sound that could be heard for an uncomfortably long time was the panting breaths of Ruth and Millicent. A ghastly thud cut through the silence as Curtis' body finally succumbed to gravity and made landfall, his body lying limply across the beaten path.

"Does anyone *else* want to test their fate today? What are you motherfuckers doing here? When is enough going to be enough? Once one of us women are dead at your hands because you've spent more time making love to a bottle than you have your wife? This is absurd. Move out of our way. We have *business* to tend to, as you fools say."

The women did not wait for the other men to abide. They trampled directly over Curtis' lifeless body and through the door. On any other day, what happened next would've seemed like a great deal of fun to even the most mundane of people, but certainly the women were not there for some kind of fun little rendezvous–they were there to send a message and make their point very clear.

One by one, shelves of liquor were ripped from their respective places on the walls, shattering the glasses and bottles with ease. Kegs were split wide open, spilling their contents into mead-filled rivers across the floorboards.

"Stop this right this instant! I demand you leave this place immediately! The cops are on their way here now, Millicent. Take your women and LEAVE!"

"Oh Tom, we will not be doing that. The cops? They won't do a damned thing either. What you all are doing here is no more legal than what I am, what *we* are. If I'm going down, you're coming with me, you bastard," Millicent retorted to the brawny man.

The crew of women continued on their warpath through the hidden room, flipping bar stools, smashing signs and artwork, essentially destroying anything tangible in sight. Shrapnel from the glass was flying in every direction; it was nearly impossible not to be impaled by at least some of it. The women sent their rocks flying through the drywall and wooden walls and chipped at those encased in cement. Light fixtures were ripped from their placements, one of which was yanked down and further used as its own dual purpose weapon. Tom and a man that Millie nor Ruth knew immediately had led the momentous effort by the men to try and intervene and stop the women to no avail. The men were treated promptly to two more of Ruth's rogue bullets.

When the unknown man fell to the floor grasping at his stomach where he'd been shot, one of the quietest and most meek of the women stepped forward to exact her revenge that no one saw coming. She dug her bare hands into the wound, starting at just her fingertips and savagely ripping the sides until she was wrist deep in his intestines, dragging them out of his torso. The man didn't stand a chance against Susie's brutality. His screams faded just as quickly as they came on.

"Do you…. *know* … this man, Susie?" Ruth asked with a puzzled look of intrigue across her face.

"Oh I know him, alright. While your husbands were busy battering you all and getting drunk, I came home early from a vacation at my sister's to this man asleep naked in bed with my husband, Robbie. When I confronted Robbie about it, he was too damn drunk to remember where he even met the guy or how he got into *our* bed, NAKED!"

The revelation caused more than just the women to gasp. Some of the lucky, untouched men covered their mouths in shock as well.

From behind the door, sirens could be heard in the distance approaching the building from the north and the south.

Connie reached beneath her apron, retrieving a flask from her waistband, and emptied its brown contents onto the floor. She lit a match, and before tossing it to the ground, she yelled out to the women, "RUN!" before flicking the torched stick into the nearby puddle.

The cops encroached on the premises just as the women retreated from the building one by one.

A nod from the first officer and a "What seems to be the problem here, ladies?" could be heard before the flames licked the outer walls and smoke escaped from each crack and crevice of the building.

"Nothing, officer. You go on and have yourself a good day now, you hear? And I'd stay out of there. Places like those are bad news," Millie replied almost teasingly as she attempted to shoulder past the officer.

The officer who'd just spoken to Millie wrapped his muscular arms around her, restraining her and her escape. A few of the women did manage to flee to the horses and depart the area, though a few women stayed spewing their injustices and grievances to the policemen who gave zero regard to their pleas. A second officer approached from behind Millie and secured a set of steel handcuffs around her wrists. As they sat her down, they also bound three other women in the same way, positioning them on the sidewalk curb side by side out front of the outdated building.

"You are under arres-"

"We have no regrets. We are the Tiverton Titty Toting Temperance Totality, and we haven't any regrets for what occurred here today. Our only regret is that we did not make it further, we did not successfully destroy more of these cruel and lawless establishments. But listen close to me when I say, we are not done here. Today marks a new beginning for the women in this town. We stand united. We will not be quieted by the men in this community any more."

"That's enough, ladies. Let's go. There's a nice cold shower waiting for you down at the jail, and a nice cold beer waiting for me at home. The longer you take, the longer I'll be forced away from it. Now move it."

Months passed, and three seasons came and went before Millicent, Connie, Ruth, Susie and two others were released from the jail. But they weren't out for long. The women vowed to make their point, and make their point they did. By the end of the year, not a one of the women had a marriage left to speak of, the speakeasies in town were decimated and reduced to ashes, and the women made a name for themselves within the jailhouse. They were a force to be reckoned with, but through trial and fire, they became a force greater than that of their husbands or the alcohol they consumed. In fact, for the next few years, the women would spend more time locked up behind bars than they would out on the streets as free women. By the time they were released indefinitely, alcohol was no longer prohibited, and bars and saloons were thriving again. Pity be the women, the government's policies win again at the expense of the nation.

4. Clockwork
D.L. Winchester (1940 – 1960's)

The young woman pretended to ignore the limping man approaching her desk. He was about her age, which was unusual. Most men of their generation were in Europe or the Pacific, fighting the Axis Powers.

"Excuse me," he said when he reached the desk.

She looked up. "Can I help you?" There was a touch of hostility in her voice. Why was he here when people she cared about were overseas doing their duty, fighting and dying?

"I saw your ad for the night watchman position and wanted to apply."

"Oh." She made a show of sneering at him. "I'm not sure an invalid like yourself would be able to handle the physical demands of the job. Besides, Mr. Porter is unlikely to consider someone who avoided serving their country. He's extremely patriotic."

The man's face flushed red. He opened his mouth to speak then stopped himself. Reaching in his pocket, he pulled out a small case and sat it on the desk.

With a slight frown, the woman reached across the

desk for the case. She opened it and stared inside, then snapped the case closed and pushed it back to him, her face flushing from embarrassment.

"Please have a seat, mister…"

"Hanover. Eli Hanover."

She nodded, trying not to look at him. "Mr. Porter will be with you shortly."

"Mr. Hanover," Porter was a tall, rotund man with a receding hairline. He came around his desk with his hand outstretched. "I'm so sorry for how Miss Delvaney greeted you. She's lost two brothers and her fiancé in the last year, and she's not fond of men who shirk their duty."

"I understand," Hanover said. "I'm starting to get used to it."

"A well-built young man like yourself, people are naturally curious why you're still here, even with your limp," Porter gestured to a chair as he went back behind his desk. "Miss Delvaney said you had two medals. How'd you get them?"

The younger man shook his head. "I don't like talking about that, or even thinking about it, really."

Porter nodded. "Good answer. The only men who like talking about their medals are politicians. They aren't worth having around."

Hanover smiled. "I can agree with that. When they gave me the Navy Cross, I almost threw it off the ship on my way home. Someone else got one at the same time I did, and they were parading all over the hospital ship with their chest stuck out, showing it to anyone who cared to look. Like a piece of ribbon and metal made them hot shit. Most of the boys who deserve medals don't survive to get them, in my opinion."

A nod. "I understand. My granddad was at Cold Harbor in the Civil War. In his first fight, he went across the field at the Confederate earthworks and came back without his left arm and right leg."

"Wow," Eli's eyebrows raised.

Porter shook his head. "He was one of the lucky ones. Granddad always said he didn't do it for a medal; he did it because that's what the orders were. But you didn't come to talk about history, you came for a job." Porter picked up a piece of paper off his desk. "I hope you're not disappointed. It's just a night watchman's post, nothing terribly exciting."

Eli smiled. "I've had all the excitement I can handle. I'm not too picky about what the position is. With my leg gone, there's not too many places willing to take a chance on me. I just need something to keep me occupied, so I can feel like I'm doing something."

Porter nodded. "Shame about your leg."

"I traded it for a squad of Japs trying to overrun my battalion. It was a small price to pay," Hanover replied.

"Fair enough," Porter said, trying not to feel embarrassed. Hanover had probably received plenty of sympathy, and he was obviously tired of it. "I've got a factory that closed when the war started. It made grandfather clocks, and because of the rationing, we can't get the supplies to run it. We offered it to the War Production Board, but they couldn't use it, so it's waiting for the war to end.

Lately, folks have been saying they see shadows inside, like people are moving around in there. It's probably just drifters or homeless folks looking for a place to get out of the elements, but I've got to stamp it out."

Hanover nodded. "I reckon I can handle it."

For a moment, Porter was struck by the wrongness of it, Hanover having to take a menial job as a night watchman to feel useful. Then he realized all the people who had rejected Eli had done him a favor.

"When can you start?"

The next evening, Eli met Miss Delaney at the loading dock of the Poplar Clock Works.

"I'm sorry for how I treated you the other day," she began. "It was rude."

"It was understandable," Eli replied. "You said what a lot of people think. I've seen the looks from people wondering why I'm here while the person they love is off at war. The worst are from the ones like you, who've felt the pain of loss. There's a hatred in their eyes. They wish I'd died instead of their loved one."

Delvaney nodded, and a tear rolled down her face. "That's what I thought when I saw you. It's been almost a year, and I still think that when I see someone Mike's age."

"Mike was your fiancé?"

Another nod, and another tear.

Eli remembered a Mike, a blond kid barely out of high school who'd been too slow jumping in a foxhole when a Zero strafed their position.

Delvaney took a deep breath. "My fiancé wasn't a hero like you, Mr. Hanover. He was a truck driver in North Africa. One day he got lost, went down the wrong road, and got stuck in the desert trying to turn around. By the time someone found him, he'd been in the heat for too long. Heatstroke. Just as fatal as the bullets flying a few miles away."

Eli sighed. "Miss Delvaney, Mike's just as much of a hero as I am. We all had a job to do, the only difference between Mike and I is some fool officer thought I could inspire others to do what I did. And please, call me Eli."

"Caroline," Delvaney offered a small smile. She was very pretty, with shoulder-length brown hair and dark brown eyes. "I've got your keys here. Just patrol the grounds once in a while and make your presence known. Other than that, sit, read, find something to keep yourself awake until dawn."

He smiled. "Maybe I'll build a clock or two."

She laughed, and Eli felt better. When his skin brushed hers as he took the keys, he felt a spark of attraction, but tried to push it aside.

She was still recovering from the war, just like him.

Eli entered the plant through a small door on the loading dock. There were four large loading bays, but Eli didn't think he could get them open on his own.

The door opened into a large warehouse. A few clocks in boxes were against one of the walls, with three hand trucks next to them. Other than that, the room was empty.

There was a double door at the far end of the room. Eli went through it and found the production floor. Workbenches filled with tools and parts sat waiting for someone to return to them.

On the table closest to him was an almost completed clock, missing only the face to cover the gears and wheels that made up the works. Around the room were more clocks in various states of assembly.

There was another set of double doors on the other end, and Eli approached them. "Supply" was painted on the door in block letters. Eli pushed them open and found himself in a room parallel to the warehouse. It was narrower, with rows of shelves reaching out from the walls.

He looked at some of the shelves, using his flashlight to read the handwritten labels: "Wood stain," "#7 gear," "pendulum mechanism." Everything had its place. If it wasn't for the layer of dust covering the inside of the building, he thought, they could come in and start making clocks tomorrow.

Shining his flashlight around, he saw the footprints he had left in the dust. Something else caught his eye, and he dropped onto his remaining knee for a closer look.

It was a print in the dust, small and round, like someone had poked the floor with a rod or a cane. Looking around, he saw hundreds of similar marks on the floor, some fresh, some starting to fill with dust.

But his were the only footprints.

Wondering what could have made the marks, Eli got to his feet and walked toward another set of doors. He went through them and found himself back in the warehouse next to the loading dock.

Shining his light around, he saw more of the marks in here, but no footprints besides his own path from the door to the production floor.

As Eli walked back to the production floor, he realized something was odd. Aside from his own footprints, there were no signs another human had been in the building since they closed the doors.

Where was the evidence of intruders?

Two nights passed, with no sign of intruders. Eli couldn't even find a way they could be getting in—the doors were locked tight, and there weren't any broken windows they could use to sneak through.

As he walked the grounds outside the factory, he looked for other signs of human presence. But there was nothing—no litter, no temporary shelters leaning against the cinderblock wall. It was pristine.

The third night, he took a smoke break in his car and fell asleep. When he woke up, he looked toward the factory and saw a light in the window of the production floor.

Getting out of his car, he hobbled back to the loading dock and entered the warehouse. Hurrying through it, he pushed open the door to the production area and found…

No one.

It was empty. The lights were off, there were no new footprints on the floor, and no sign of anyone.

Eli walked through the supply room, then went back into the warehouse. He stopped, looking at the wall where the completed clocks were standing in their crates.

How many had been there before?

He hadn't counted, but he'd swear there were two new ones. He walked closer and saw two of the box tops weren't covered in dust like the others.

But that was impossible.

He shook his head, then made another lap of the building, finding nothing. Eli went back to the warehouse and counted the completed clocks.

Eighteen crates.

Now if more appeared, he'd know.

The next morning, he stopped at Mr. Porter's office on the way home to pick up his paycheck. He'd left the factory at dawn and was sitting in the hall waiting when Caroline arrived.

"I'm so sorry," she said, digging in her purse to find the keys. "Have you been waiting long?"

"No ma'am," Eli lied, getting to his feet.

"I told you, my name is Caroline." She found the keys and opened the door.

"Sorry, force of habit," Eli said as he followed her into the office.

She laughed. "Mike did the same thing the first time he was on leave." Caroline paused, looking away from him. Eli put a hand on her shoulder.

"It's okay to talk about him. It's how you heal."

"I know," she said. "But it hurts."

"Yeah, it does. But not talking doesn't make it hurt less."

Caroline turned toward him, and he saw the tears on her face. But she gave him a soft smile. "That makes sense, even if I don't want it to."

Eli reached out and took her left hand. Holding it up, he nodded toward the ring still on her finger. "Moving on doesn't mean forgetting."

She nodded. "Thank you."

He smiled. "Dr. Eli at your service."

That got a laugh. "Do you have any plans for the weekend?"

Eli shook his head. "Just getting caught up on sleep. Maybe I'll catch a movie or something."

"Want to get together?"

His eyes widened, and she smiled. "It doesn't have to be a date or anything. I just thought, maybe you need to talk as much as I do."

Eli smiled. "How about dinner tomorrow night?"

Eli strolled into the warehouse Sunday night whistling a chipper tune. His evening with Caroline had been better than expected, one of the few times he remembered being happy since the war began. The tingle of her goodbye kiss still lingered on his cheek.

It disappeared when he saw the crates in the warehouse.

There were new ones.

Just to be sure, he counted, and came up with twenty-one.

Eli went to the production floor and found a hammer and pry bar. Going back to the warehouse, he used the pry bar to open one of the new crates.

Inside was a grandfather clock, in pristine condition.

"What the hell?" he muttered.

A chime sounded, and he jumped back. The clock in front of him was operational, sounding the half-hour. Closing the lid, he hammered it back in place, then sat against the front of the box.

Clocks can't appear out of nowhere, he told himself.

But they are…

The next morning, Eli stopped by Porter's office on his way home.

"What a pleasant surprise," Caroline said. Her hair was in a neat updo, and traces of makeup showed on her face. She'd changed from the grieving woman he'd met a few weeks before.

"I just had a quick question about the factory," he said, smiling at her.

"Is that all?" She pretended to pout. "I'd hoped you had a good enough time this weekend to have another reason to stop by."

"There may have been ulterior motives," Eli's eyes twinkled. "You busy this weekend?"

Caroline smiled. "I am now. What was your other question?"

"Were there any clocks left in the warehouse when the factory closed?"

She shook her head. "Nope. Mr. Porter sold them all. He said if we tried to store them until the war was over, if vermin didn't get into them, there'd be a leak in the roof or something else to destroy them."

"And there weren't any left at all?"

She shook her head, then pointed across the room. "That was the last one. Mr. Porter decided to put it here to remind us we can do more than make war machines."

Eli nodded, trying to process this. If the warehouse had been empty, someone was making clocks in the factory.

"Why are you so curious about the warehouse?" Caroline asked.

"Because there's twenty-one new clocks in it."

Caroline's eyes narrowed. "That's impossible."

"You'd think," Eli shrugged. "The weird thing is, there were only eighteen when I left Friday."

She paused, then shook her head. "Are you suggesting someone is sneaking into the factory to build clocks?"

He shrugged again. "I don't know what to think. All I know is there were new clocks in the warehouse last night that weren't there when I left Friday."

Caroline leaned back in her chair. "That's…I don't even know what that is. I'll have to tell Mr. Porter, but you go home and rest. I want you ready for the weekend."

Porter was waiting for him when Eli got to the warehouse that night.

"Making clocks in your spare time?" he called as Eli approached. Eli grinned as Porter laughed at his own joke. "Maybe some folks forgot to pick up their clock before we closed down. It was hectic, the early days of the war. I've got a list of the most recent orders to check the serial numbers. We'll get to the bottom of this!"

Eli unlocked the warehouse door and held it open for Porter. The older man went inside and walked over to the boxes.

"The serial number is in the upper left hand corner of the crate. At her peak, this factory could turn out five thousand clocks per year! It's six digits, the first two are the year, and the last four are the production number. We closed down on the hundred and nineteenth clock of 1942, so that one would be 42-0119..."

Eli had stopped listening and was looking at a new crate that hadn't been there when he left that morning.

The serial number read 43-0022.

Porter looked at Eli, then followed his eyes.

"That's impossible," Porter whispered. "We haven't made a new clock in over a year."

"I didn't notice it until yesterday," Eli said. "I thought they were supposed to be here."

"And you secure your keys when you're not here?" Porter asked.

Eli nodded. "Yes sir. If they're not in my pocket, they're on my dresser."

"I guess that brings me back to my original question," Porter said. "Are you making clocks in your spare time?"

Eli shook his head. "No sir, I wouldn't have the first clue as to how."

"And when you first arrived and noticed there were clocks in the warehouse, you didn't think to ask anyone about them?"

Another shake of the head. "Not until I realized there were more. I figured they were supposed to be there."

Porter shook his head. "Jesus Christ. I can't decide if you're naive or incompetent, Hanover."

"What?" Eli felt his cheeks starting to burn in anger.

"You're the damn watchman, and someone's making clocks under your nose!"

"They're not doing it while I'm here!" Eli shot back.

"I'm not sure what happens while you're here! For all I know you're kicking back and sleeping the night away while God knows who is banging away in the workshop building clocks!" Porter yelled.

"That's stupid!" Eli yelled back. "Why the hell

would someone build clocks pro bono?"

"I don't know, but since you didn't bother to figure it out before you got Miss Delvaney wound up, I'm damn sure going to find out!" Porter stomped off toward the workshop.

"You do that," Eli hissed at his retreating back.

Porter whirled around. "What did you say?"

"I said I quit." Eli took his keys out of his pocket and took off the ring Caroline had given him. Throwing the keys on the ground, he stomped out of the warehouse, not trusting himself to open his mouth again.

The next afternoon, Eli woke up to someone knocking on his door. He threw on some clothes and opened the door to find Caroline standing there.

"Have you seen Mr. Porter?" she asked.

"Not since I quit last night."

"What?" She pushed past him into his apartment. "Why?"

"He couldn't decide if I was naive or incompetent. But I knew he was a jackass."

Caroline laughed, a nervous chuckle. "I guess

something was up with the clocks you found."

Eli nodded. "They all have serial numbers from this year. Porter basically accused me of letting someone build clocks under my nose."

Caroline shook her head. "Jesus. I don't know what to do, Eli. He didn't turn up for work this morning, and he's not at his house or any of his other businesses, so I wondered if he was at the clock factory, but I don't have keys…"

Eli put his hand on her shoulder. "I'll go check and see if he's there."

"Really?" She reached out and grabbed his hand. "Thank you, thank you."

Eli got to the warehouse to find the doors locked but Mr. Porter's car in the same spot where it had been parked the night before. Looking around, Eli decided to shimmy up the drainpipe to the ventilation fan. It wasn't easy, but he managed to squeeze past the blades and into the warehouse.

Moving across the rafters, Eli looked down to see a new crate in the warehouse.

Then he heard something, the ping of metal

striking metal from the workshop. He continued along the rafters, one beam at a time, until he passed the wall and could look down into the work area.

"Jesus," he whispered.

Porter was on a table, his skin split down the middle and pulled aside. His ribcage had been cracked open, and his organs were in a pile on the floor. A strange creature made of gears and clockwork was stuffing a pendulum into Porter's chest cavity.

The creature stood on six spindly poles attached to gears that allowed it to scamper around like a spider. Its hands were made of gloves from the supply room, no doubt stuffed with mechanical parts that let them move like human hands. The body was a small wooden box, unstained, cradled atop the legs. Looking closer, Eli realized the creature's parts could collapse into the box, leaving it unremarkable.

He couldn't remember seeing a box the night he saw the light in the workshop, but he'd bet one was there.

Eli started to back across the rafters toward the ventilation shaft, but he hit something with his foot. It dropped to the floor with a clatter, and he saw the creature spin toward the noise, then lift its body toward him.

Then it sounded a deep clang.

"Shit!"

Eli heard scurrying, and he turned and crawled across the rafters. Beneath him, he saw more of the creatures coming to life, scampering up the walls to his hiding place.

How can something with no eyes look at me? Eli wondered as he moved across the rafters. Beneath him, one of the creatures was moving toward the far wall. It flicked a switch, and the ventilation fan roared to life.

Shit.

Swinging his body down, Eli dropped from the rafters and aimed a kick at the closest creature. It flew into the wall and shattered, but as soon as it hit the floor it started piecing itself back together.

Another one ran toward Eli, and he grabbed a two-by-four leaning against the wall and swung it like a bat, knocking the creature away from him.

Eli barreled through the door into the workshop, slipping the two-by-four through the door handles to hold them closed.

The creature working on Porter looked up as Eli looked around for a solution. A window was on the far wall, and he ran for it. He grabbed an iron pipe and got ready to swing it, to smash the window and dive outside.

Would the creatures follow him?

He never found out.

Before he reached the window, strong hands grabbed his ankles, sending him tumbling to the floor. Eli tried to scream, but a leather glove pressed over his mouth. He kicked and squirmed, trying to break away, but more hands grabbed him, lifting him off the ground and carrying him toward the table.

As he got closer, he smelled the decay of Porter, and realized the same thing would happen to him.

Eli didn't want to die, but he didn't think he had a choice.

But he was sure his conversion, like Porter's, would go like clockwork.

5. What a Trip
David Hardy (1960 – 1970's)

Groovin' to the Beat

Black sharp lettering laid against the bright red background caught my eye as I passed by Stephano's Pizzeria on the other side of the street. Taped to the inside of the display window hung the flyer I had been waiting to see for months. Against the vibrant background a single white bird perched atop a guitar. The black bold letters across the top read, "3 Days of Peace and Music,".

Motherfucking Woodstock had officially been announced.

Sprinting across the two-lane blacktop, ignoring the beeping horn of an angry Mustang driver, I nearly careened against the window before I had a chance to come to a stop. Janis Joplin, Creedence Clearwater, Grateful Dead, and when I read the name Jimi Hendrix, I almost collapsed.

My heart stopped when I saw the ticket prices. Who could fathom $7 for 1 day, $13 for 2 days and $18 for all three days. It would be damn near impossible to pay $18 for all three days with my salary. I'd have to work all summer long just to save up enough to go. Had I not depleted my savings the month prior by buying a pound of the best grass California had to offer, I would be in the clear. But Humboldt County primo wasn't something you passed up, so I dropped the coin for a brick.

Pulling out my coin pouch, I counted out a total of fifty cents to my name. Pissed at my misfortune, I pulled an old Pall Mall pack I kept my re-rolls in from my pocket and lit the sweet tobacco that I'd cut with some of the best grass you could find.

Glancing back at the flyer, I cursed before making my way back to Katz Music Emporium up the street. Scotty should be working, and where there was Scotty, Lisa was in tow. Pulling another drag on my cig, I huffed out the plume of smoke while rolling through my head the ideas of how I was going to be able to afford a bus ticket, a ticket to the festival, and let's not even think about the amount of grass I would need to bring. Then there was food and drinks that would need to be considered. Being in mid-August, the weather would be beautiful and perfect for the little tent I saved up for, which meant I wouldn't need to find a place to stay or spend money to have a roof over my head.

Grabbing the brass handle to Katz, I yanked the

door open to a flurry of rhythmic guitar riffs that sang to the soul. The way Hendrix spoke through his guitar soothed something inside me that I couldn't put my finger on.

"Hey Man," I heard just loud enough to make out that it was Scotty from behind the counter.

"Hey Man," I responded, stubbing out my cigarette on the heel of my Chucks. "Vibing some Hendrix today?"

"Yeah, man," Scotty said. "Ever since I saw he was announced for Woodstock, man, I couldn't help myself."

"Right on! I passed by Steph's just a bit ago and saw the flyer. Can you believe the lineup? So many good artists. The vibe is going to be out of this world," I said.

"You can say that again," Scotty said. "Lisa and I were just talking about how we could make it down there. I think it's like four hours from here."

"Have you seen the ticket prices though? That's my whole summer's savings right there," I replied. "I want to go because it's going to be the show of all shows, but those ticket prices have me pinched."

"Lisa's dad has that V-dub bus that I've been trying to buy from him forever. I thought maybe I'd take a little bit of that money to get tickets for Lisa and I. If he lets me borrow it to drive down there with her, maybe you could tag along? It'd save you some coin," he said.

"Groovy," I exclaimed. "I'm sure I can work the summer to save up for the ticket and use the bus fare money to get us some more of that primo bud from Reggie."

"Hey guys," Lisa said, closing the door to the stockroom. "Are you going to Woodstock, Jeff?"

"With a little bit of luck, the power of Hendrix, and as much grass as my lungs can handle, I should be able to make it," I replied.

"Far out! Scotty and I are going to take my dad's bus down. The best part is we can lay the seats down in the back so it's nice and flat. That way we can just sleep there all weekend long."

"Primo," I said.

"Hope that bus has good shocks," Scotty muttered.

"Scott!" Lisa snapped. "Behave, you caveman."

As I laughed at Scott's joke, he scooped Lisa into his arms faster than a bolt of lightning. While the love birds tongue wrestled, I made my exit, allowing the heavy glass door to close as Mean Mistreater by the one and only Johnny Winter blared through the music shop's speakers.

Lighting another cig, I made the trek back towards

the old railroad that ran behind my house on Jackson Road. With my mind going with the flow, Winter's tune beating in my head, I let the universe take me to the state of peace that came with inner reflection. Woodstock '69 was going to be the best thing in my life, and I was going to make it one way or another.

The Unexpected

The beat-up baby blue 1948 Ford F100 chugged through the sand of the quarry where I was ordered to pick up Jack's load of gravel. It wasn't the most well-paying job, but for $50 a week, it kept the grass flowing, food in my belly, and all my bills paid. Not to mention I didn't have to work for "the Man" in order to make a living. All my money was tax free and under the table. All I had to do was take his junker, pick up some gravel, and unload it wherever he was paid to dump it. The only stipulation he asked was not to smoke on the job. Simple enough tasks with some hard work that helped keep the munchies from wreaking havoc on my body.

With the truck bed filled, I shifted the truck into gear and slowly made my way out onto Jackson II Road to make the delivery somewhere east on Route 3. Jack said to look for the big red barn with a white tractor parked out front, which meant only one of two farms–the Dandridges, with their beautiful daughter Mary J, or The Courtlands. The latter sent a chill down my spine knowing that their son Richard would probably be home and ready to break my neck the second he saw me.

Turning onto Route 3, I drove for about fifteen minutes before I reached my destination. None other than Richard Courtland and his gang of testosterone-juiced neanderthals. Sure, he was star quarterback for the Comets, but deep down, his hatred for anything that rebelled against the normal views of modern society put a chip on his shoulder that he couldn't shake off. That directly reflected against me as I looked down at my threads. Bell bottoms and my fringe vest to match my purple tinted sunglasses.

It probably didn't help that he caught me knuckles deep in his sister while intramural basketball was going on. Cheryl Courtland was everything a man could dream of. Dark auburn hair cascaded down to her shoulders, which only accentuated her large chest. All sat atop a frame of long legs and a thick waist. A man's dream in the flesh, and at the height of our senior year, I called her mine. Well, until she got that scholarship to Harvard. It'd been two years since she left, and there was no sign of her ever coming back.

Turning down the gravel drive towards the tractor and barn, I slowed the blue junker to a halt a mere ten feet from Richard's feet.

"The fuck you doing here, hippie trash?" Richard spat.

"Hey man, I don't mean no harm. You know I work for Jack, and it just so happens I'm on this delivery, man. Just trying to make some dough this summer," I replied in the friendliest voice I could muster.

"I'm about to knead your face like dough, hippie. Get the fuck out of here," he yelled, clenching his fists at his sides.

"Richard! Get your ass back in the house and let me handle this," the gruff voice of Richard Sr. rang out.

"Yes, Pa," Richard said, defeated.

"Hey Jeff," Senior waved. "Spin that old piece of shit around and back it up to my tractor please."

Glad that my face wasn't about to be twisted into a loaf of bread, I spun the truck one hundred and eighty degrees, positioning the tailgate just right. I backed the old lumber wagon up to Senior's brand new tractor.

"Whoa, right there, Jeff. Shovel it all right there, if you don't mind," Senior directed.

"Sure thing, man. I mean, sir," I said, briskly jumping into the back of the truck where I started shoveling scoop after scoop of gravel.

"Once you're done unloading, you're free to go. I'll handle the rest of it from there," he said, letting the screen door slam shut as he walked back into the house.

Staring down at the mountain of gravel, I wished the old man would have sprung for one of them dump beds, but at the end of the day, it was an honest day's work and beat having to watch what I ate or worse, work out like some of the jocks.

Scoop after scoop, I slowly got the bed cleared out. Grabbing the broom I kept behind the seat, I swept out the back and made sure no leftover gravel had made its way onto the bumper.

"You finally done, faggot?" I heard from the house.

Spinning on my heels, I looked at Richard walking around the side of the house with two of his buddies.

"Mellow out, man.I'm done here. Just making sure the old Ford is clean before I get back on the road," I said.

"That's if you make it that far," he snickered. "Get 'em, boys."

Both brutes sprinted toward me, but not fast enough, as I slammed the door on the first guy. The sound of his fingers snapping like twigs was music to my ears. I never wanted to fight someone and never personally wanted to wish or deliver harm onto anyone. That changed the moment my life was in danger. Slamming the clutch pedal, twisting the key and yanking the gear shift down, I popped the clutch to send me on my way. Leaning forward to anticipate the lurch of a speeding pile of junk, I slammed against the steering wheel as the truck jerked backwards. The gravel peppered the undercarriage just before my ears heard the unmistakable crunch of metal against metal.

In a rush of adrenaline, I had put the fucking truck into reverse, slamming the rear end straight into Richard Senior's new tractor. The David Brown 880 was beautiful with fresh paint and not a speck of dirt on her. Over the roar of laughter, I pulled the truck forward just in time to see Richard Senior busting through the screen door.

"God damn it, you fucking idiot. Do you know what you just did?" the scream echoed right in my ear as one of the neanderthals held his broken fingers.

"What the fuck happened out here?" Senior screamed.

"This hippy piece of shit ran into your tractor," Junior laughed.

"Sir, it was an honest mistake. Those guys were running after me, and I accidentally threw it in reverse," I said.

"I ain't worried about my tractor," Senior said. "You didn't even scratch the paint. The truck on the other hand," he pointed towards the crumpled tailgate, "that's gonna cost you at least a few hundred to replace."

Staring down at the crumpled hunk of metal, I knew my dream of going to Woodstock was over.
I was completely and sincerely fucked.

Trippin' Out

My worst fear had come and gone when I reached Jack's house. There was a lot of cussing, a lot of questions, and worst of all, he wanted to search me to make sure I wasn't high. After all the chaos had settled, he wanted me to pay him back 200 dollars to fix the tailgate. Even after all of the extra deliveries I could take on, it would take until November till I could pay him back and make sure I had enough money to live on. I was royally fucked on this one, and there really was no way to get out of it.

Lighting my last cig from the pack, I crumpled the carton, tossing it into the ditch next to the old railroad I walked on back to my house. It wasn't very "save the planet" of me to do, so I huffed before I ran back to retrieve my discarded carton. I reached down to retrieve my trash and right before I stood up, a crumpled piece of paper lay tattered next to where it had landed. The dollar bill sign caught my eye, and I snatched it off the ground to read.

Need cash fast? Have an unexpected expense that has you down? No need to worry any longer. A once-in-a-lifetime opportunity is at your fingertips! Become part of a study on the effects of psychedelics.

That's right: Get paid to get high!

If you are chosen for the program, you will participate in a two-week study and walk out with a cool $250. That's right, $250 to get high for two weeks!

But wait! There's more!

Every participant will have their name entered into a secondary round where you could receive an additional $250 to help a special branch of the military with a new state-of-the-art formula to enhance recovery from battle fatigue.

Act fast, because spots are filling up quickly! Call (311-555-8674) between the hours of 7:00 AM and 7:00 PM. The last day to enter is June 4th. Don't delay. Act today!

Hands shaking, I searched my memory for the day's date. I could have sworn today was the 4th, but what if it was the 5th? If it was the latter, then there would be no way I would have a chance at solving a whole lot of my problems. Stuffing the paper into my pocket, I raced down the black pebbled railway toward my house. I needed to call that number, and I needed to get a spot on that research group.

Spinning the dial on the telephone, I rushed through the numbers while I stared at the calendar.

June 4th with a big "x" through it caused several beads of sweat to roll down my forehead. It must have been the universe's way of saying it was meant to be when the number connected. The older lady that answered the phone in a gruff voice went through the preliminary questions. By the end of the twenty-minute phone call, I was left exhausted and defeated when she placed me on a brief hold. That hold ended up being ten minutes of some elevator music that nearly drove me insane.

"Accepted," the gruff voice on the other end of the line muttered. "Report for your physical and day one of the trial at the House of Good Samaritan Hospital in Watertown, New York tomorrow no later than 9:00 AM."

"Yes ma'am," I replied before ending the call.

My Destiny had been fulfilled.

It was just meant to be.

Pulling the shoe box out from under my flower-printed couch, I pulled the lid off to reveal the heavenly bud. Pulling a zigzag from the pouch, I rolled the biggest joint I could roll with my fingers. A spark of the lighter and the sweet aroma of Humboldt Gold filled my lungs.

Allowing the bud to work its magical hand around my consciousness, I allowed my mind to drift to what it would be like to stand front row and center while Jimi Hendrix spoke with his guitar. The beat, the rhythm, and all of the little quirks that grasped your soul while it licked your consciousness mellowed me to a state of pure bliss. Relaxed, I laid down on the couch letting the haze take hold.

Tomorrow was the day.

Tomorrow was the day I would embrace my good fortune.

Poked and Prodded

It wasn't the cough that caught me off guard.

It was the beautiful, red-headed, green-eyed demon with her forked tongue, sharp tipped horns and lustrous gaze while she kneaded my balls in her hand that froze me in shock.

First it was a hit of acid and immediately followed by a taste test of various juices. The cranberry concoction nearly made me puke. Then it was on to a physical exam where they drew my blood and listened to my heartbeat and lungs before finally having me drop my pants to inspect my Mr. Gadget. All the while this red-headed demon's eyes bored into me with silent affliction.

The subsequent days of testing were much more thorough while simultaneously being a disaster.

A hit of what they called CHONO in the morning and then another two at lunch. CHONO was a type of LSD that was supposed to have an overexaggerated effect on the psyche. To say it was an over-exaggeration would be an absolute undermining of the actual trip. I've had heavy trips, bad trips, fun trips, but I've never had a trip that made me question my existence.

By day three, I felt fried. The acid left me dazed and

confused for the remainder of the day, leaving me with no other choice than to tell Jack that I was sick. He wasn't happy when I called out of work the first day, but by day three of not working, he was royally pissed.

"I'm telling ya man, I am sick as a dog," I said.

"If you don't come back to work by tomorrow, I'll have no choice but to fire you, Jeff, and I really don't want to do that," he replied.

"I know Mr. Jack, but truly, I am so sick," I said.

Lucky for me, the initial observation period was over. I could return to work, which would keep Jack off my back, and all I had to do was wait for the phone call that I had been selected for the second part of the study. A study that I wasn't 100% sure I wanted to be a part of. The fact Woodstock was fast approaching was the only thing that gave me hope.

It had been three weeks since the initial study at Good Samaritan when I received a check in the mail. I immediately ran to the bank to cash it, wrote a check to Woodstock Music Box to mail out, and then ran directly to Jack's to pay off my debt for my mishap with ole blue.

Flipping through my hemp billfold, I counted out the $20 I had left to my name. That meant I could get some more Humboldt Gold from Reggie or spring for a bit of Thai Stick to hold me over till the next time Jack paid me. Settling on what Reggie offered, I finished my rounds by scoring a dime from him.

Halfway down my gravel drive, with a cig in my mouth and a bag of primo, I stopped dead in my tracks when I caught sight of the old olive drab Jeep parked in my driveway.

Property of Camp Drum was spray painted in block letters across the side of the door. Upon getting closer, I could barely make out the green uniform of a soldier walking around my little trailer. Waving at the soldier, I caught his attention, setting him on course to meet me in the driveway.

"Jeff Russo," the man said.

"Yeah, I'm Jeff," I responded, noticing that there was no identification on his fatigues.

Producing a crisp white envelope from his breast pocket, he handed it over for me to take. Handwritten on the front was a single word, 'Classified'. My heart immediately jumped into my throat. I had been chosen, and I knew it.

"You report at 0600 hours. Main Gate 1. The letter contains the rest of the information you need. Have a good day, sir," the man said.

Jumping into the Jeep, he reversed and drove back down the driveway without a single glance into the side mirror. Ripping open the envelope as fast as my fingers could manage, I yanked the white letter out.

Sure enough, arrive at six in the morning at the front gate. Ask for Dr. Millard Rausch. Upon arrival, you will be stripped of clothes, jewelry, and any personal effects. That didn't sound promising, but it was what it was. Payment will be delivered in cash at the end of testing. Glancing back at the top, I realized in horror what I'd have to give in order to go. Date of testing, August 12th, 13th, and 14th. Woodstock dates, August 15th, 16th, and 17th. Now I was truly fucked if this study was worse than the first.

Turtles All The Way Down

Piss-pouring rain cascaded against my naked flesh, snapping me out of the trance-like state. The wad of 20s I held in my hand was my only form of concealment from the pelting rain. A sharp crack of lightning illuminated the sky, sending a reverberating crash of thunder to finally kick my ass into high gear. Rushing to the front door of my little trailer, I ran inside to only be immediately hit with the most glorious smell known to man.

Primo weed.

I inhaled sharply at the intoxicating scent, sending the smoke deep into my lungs. Looking around, I realized Lisa was perched on my couch with both legs propped on my coffee table while Scotty divulged himself between her legs. The lapping of tongue against wet flesh sent a jolt of hunger both to my stomach and to my appendage between my legs. In the blink of an eye, I had my rod buried deep down Lisa's throat while she cried out in ecstasy.

The surge of my orgasm painted the back of her throat, which only enhanced the sensation when I felt her swallow around my cock. The constriction of her esophagus sent a ripple of pleasure that caused me to shutter. Flopping back on the couch in my post-orgasmic clarity, I watched Scotty unload a cataclysmic load of orgasm onto Lisa's chest.

Thank the universe for Free Love.

"Jeff, why are you soaking wet?" Lisa asked.

"Well, you see. I…" I paused. "I don't really know."

"You haven't been home for three days, and we are leaving in about thirty minutes to head to Woodstock. Are you even ready?" Scotty asked.

"Yeah man, I had to get cash," I said, waving towards the stack of 20s on the coffee table.

"Right on! Well, go get dressed man. We got the bus loaded and ready to go," Scotty said, yanking Lisa off the couch. "Plenty more of that to cum."

Jumping off the couch, I ran to my bedroom to throw on a fresh pair of jeans. I remember packing my bags before I left to go to Camp Drum, but I didn't remember much past stripping naked at the gate and getting my "initial hit," as the doctor called it. I'm not sure if it was the black beard or the eye patch, but either way, the pirate-looking doctor had given me what I felt was a small hit from some sort of inhaler. The effects were immediate, as I don't recall ever starting the three-day study.

Throwing my bags in the back of the bus, I hopped in while Scotty got behind the wheel and Lisa jumped in to ride shotgun.

"Four hours till we are there, Jeff! You ready?" Scotty called out from the front.

"Right on, man! Let's get this bus on the road. I'm gonna take me a quick nap, but wake me when we get to the next gas station so I can roll us some joints," I said, patting the bag where I had a full ounce of the best bud known to man.

Curling my backpack with the duffle bag strapped to it into the corner of the seat, I laid my head down to try and catch some sleep. The problem presented itself in visions of my time at Camp Drum.

First it was the urethral sounding Dr. Rausch administered. The long, pencil-thick metal rod was lubed up before being inserted into depths of my body where no one or anything had ever gone before. The next flash of memory resulted in a stomach regurgitation spasm when I remembered the taste of the tar-like liquid that was administered down my throat with a syringe. The thick, viscous syrup tasted like rotted meat drizzled in honey.

What jolted me upright was the memory of the gas chamber. The immediate reflexive jerk to inhale sharply due to the inability to breathe snapped me awake quicker than the fuzz knocking on my door.

The smell of rotted vegetation clogged my nose as I remembered the chemical smell mixed with fertilizer that was brought on from the canister of Trioxin they dropped into the room.

"Jesus, man! You okay back there,? Scotty said, nearly swerving off the road from my violent outburst.

"Yeah, man," I said. "Bad nightmare. Thought we ran out of bud." I chuckled, hoping they wouldn't catch on to my state of unease.

"Man, that would be more than a nightmare," Lisa laughed.

"Speaking of bud, roll us one up, man," Scotty chirped.

Grabbing my bag, I pulled out the album that I used to roll. Luckily, Reggie had found some of the good shit. None of that shake that needed to be gone through from all the stems and seeds. There were still seeds in this batch, but the buds were thick with flower instead of the thick branches.

With the joint rolled, I sparked the lighter and inhaled deeply. The smooth, aromatic smoke coursing through the air like pillows of clouds. Handing off the stick, I watched as the bus slowly became engulfed.

"Don't smoke weed, don't do acid, and *definitely* don't have intercourse for the next forty-eight hours. The Trioxin may have serious consequences we are

not aware of yet. That is why you signed a waiver,"
Dr. Rausch's voice called out in my mind.

Another Piece of My Heart

Fried couldn't even begin to explain how my brain felt. Halfway through the Jimi Hendrix set, I popped another hit of acid. The train of spiritual flow coursed through my body as "Foxy Lady" blared through the speakers. We were so close to the stage I could see the perspiration pour out of his forehead.

Dazed, I watched on as his magical set concluded with an encore performance of "Hey Joe."

Wrapped up in each other's arms, I tagged along as Scotty played grab ass with Lisa in front of me. We had been up all night dropping acid, smoking bud, and periodically shuffling our way to a more secluded spot to empty a load down Lisa's throat.

It wasn't till about the beginning of Hendrix's set that I started to feel a bit off. I chalked it up to indigestion from not eating. Paying a couple of bucks for a burger some guy grilled, I immediately scarfed it down and knew something was wrong. The craving for food was only intensified. I figured dropping more acid would satiate the need for food, but it never went away.

"Hey man, I'm getting really hungry," I called out to the two love birds.

"Glad I'm not the only one," Lisa turned with a

smile on her face. "Yes, I want cock, but I really need some food. I feel like I'm starving."

"Don't we have a bunch of beef jerky still in the van?" Scotty asked.

"Oh shit, we do," I said.

It was supposed to be for the ride home, but I was sure we could grab some more food on the way. As soon as realization hit that we had food, Lisa darted towards the bus where we parked and set up camp. Yanking the door wide open, she jumped inside to grab the remaining beef jerky. Dividing up the bag, Lisa and I devoured our share while Scotty set his to the side and lit a joint. The meat sticks were tasteless to my palate, which I thought was strange, but it took the edge off the hunger cramps. When all the jerky was consumed, Lisa ripped her top off, exposing herself.

"Come on boys," she said, curling her index finger toward us.

Stubbing out the joint, Scotty immediately dropped his jeans to the ground before crawling up into the makeshift bed of the bus. It was only a matter of seconds before the sound of flesh slapping flesh began. The sound of two fleshbags going at it recoiled in my stomach.

I ran to the other side of the bus to vomit the

undigested jerky and stomach bile. The retching wouldn't stop no matter what I tried. Even after all the contents of my stomach were unloaded onto the grass while the sun glared down on my back, I felt the need to vomit some more. The shriek of an orgasm sounded within the bus as Lisa screamed her lungs out from the brutal onslaught of Scotty's cock.

The next scream wasn't an orgasm, but it was definitely Scotty's voice. Running back around the bus, dry heaving as I went, I stopped dead in my tracks at the sight before me. Scotty was standing up with Lisa between his legs in what I could only assume was a blowjob in mid progress. When Scotty fell backwards, the true horror was revealed. Scotty's appendage was held in Lisa's hand, and she was eating it like a corn dog. A snap of her gnashing teeth and another glob of flesh disappeared behind her lips.

"You fucking bitch," I screamed.

Charging her, I tackled her to the ground where I ripped the cock out of her hands. Shoving the remaining globule of flesh into my mouth, I chewed while I relished the sweet taste of Scotty's bloody cock.

"More," I screamed.

Lurching towards his fallen corpse, I dug into his chest, trying my hardest to get to his heart. His heart where all the life force would be contained. It wasn't a need or a desire. It was a drive to feed the insatiable monster inside my brain.

"More," I screamed, ripping flesh from bone.

Diving straight into his chest cavity, I yanked the morsel of meat from its resting spot.

MORE

MORE

MORE

"Jeff!!! Wake up," the scream beside me echoed.

Immediately jumping up from where I lay, I took in my surroundings.

Room with four walls.

A ceiling.

A bed.

Covers.

Glancing down, I saw I was wearing shorts and a T-shirt over my rotund belly. Clawing at my face, I felt blood. So much blood. Slamming the switch to the bedside table light, I looked at my hands. Clear liquid coated my fingers and palms. Spit or snot, I wasn't sure, but not a single speck of blood.

"Jeff, what the fuck is the matter with you?" the dark-haired beauty asked.

"Go back to bed, Cheryl. I just had a nightmare is all. A really, really bad nightmare," I said, turning off the light.

Pulling the covers up to my neck, I calmed my breathing, hoping sleep would find me fast. I needed sleep.

More sleep.

More.

6. Amaze Your Friends, Terrify Your Enemies
Brennan LaFaro (1970 – 1980's)

TUESDAY

What a beautiful day, a perfect day.

Those words looped through Arnie McGuire's head as he skipped down the beautiful, perfect sidewalk, waving at anyone he passed. Forget about the tufts of grass growing through each crack like old Mr. Harrison's ear hair. Arnie snickered to himself as he passed Mr. Harrison, who glared from behind a cigarette balanced carefully on his lower lip as he washed his gold Ford Pinto. In the next yard, Mrs. Cassidy pruned a bed of her prize-winning roses. She peered over the top of her sunglasses and tipped Arnie a wink. He smiled back, trying to keep his eyes north of her ample bosom. That's what his mom always called Mrs. Cassidy's non-floral display. Still, the smile he returned was genuine and barely related to the inverted mountain range.

The smile was because today was the day.

As he neared 72 Walthery Ave, his breath hitched and excitement seized his limbs, pulling him to a stop. The front gate to his home stood open. Mr. Holley, the mailman, trotted down the porch steps, short blue shorts and too much pale leg showing. He slid sideways through the open gate and gently clicked it shut behind him.

"Is it here? Did it come?"

A placating smile winded onto Mr. Holley's face. "And what exactly would *it* be?"

"Real Ghost!" shouted Arnie.

Mr. Holley playfully stumbled backward and clutched his chest. He mopped a make-believe patch of sweat from his forehead, then leaned forward and spoke in a conspiratorial tone. "You know, I recall leaving a package on the doorstep, but blast my memory, I just can't seem to remember what it said on the label." He patted Arnie's untidy mop of red hair and jerked his head toward the McGuire's home.

Arnie squeaked out something like "Thank you" then zipped away, practically leaving a trail of smoke in his wake. Hopping the three rickety, wooden steps, Arnie skidded to a stop, sending up a spray of dust and splinters. Atop the worn doormat—woven strands of faded earthtones trying to pass for a rug—sat a shoebox-sized parcel. Easing forward,

Arnie held out his hands, wriggled his fingers like an intrepid explorer who'd unearthed treasure, then snatched the package.

There. On the label.

Real Ghost!

And right above the return address:

Amaze your friends, Terrify your enemies

Show and tell.

Three little words that sent a shiver down the spine of every fourth grade student at Hobson Elementary. Maybe the entire country. The pressure to choose the right item had brought better kids than Arnie McGuire to their knees, forced them to miss their 8:30 p.m. bedtime while their parents cobbled a last-minute project together. Something cool, unique, original. An unveiling to make the whole class gasp, and even Kara Finnegan smile and take notice.

Of course if you flubbed it, brought in something babyish, they'd all laugh at you. And God forbid you showed up with the same thing as another kid.

Arnie shuddered just thinking about it. He pictured

Mickey Willis's freckled face, balanced between a scowl and a laugh, pointing at Arnie before he turned to the rest of the class to make sure they were laughing, too.

And Mrs. Carey expected all of her students to come up with a new idea every month. The first Friday of October loomed large on Arnie's calendar.

It had been doing exactly that two weeks ago when he picked up an issue of *The Tomb of Dracula*. Issue 66 with Drac surrounded by a horde of purple beasts and grass-green zombies. He struggled to focus with the impending show and tell weighing on his mind, flipping the pages with reckless abandon until he found himself staring at an advertisement just inside the back cover.

A frowning specter drawn in the style of Gene Colan, its body white with black and dark blue outlines, making even the light appear dark. The ghost wore a jagged frown below empty eyes. Even after twenty-something pages of vampires and zombies, it gave him the creeps while simultaneously drawing a smile across his face. At the top of the ad, in the same blood-drip font as the cover page, it read:

Real Ghost!

Amaze your friends, Terrify your enemies

"Perfect," whispered Arnie.

Up in his room, alone. Light on, curtains open. No, curtains closed. The package sat on his bed, waiting while he arranged everything just right.

Bedroom door open. The house was empty, another hour at least before Dad got home from work, before Mom finished grocery shopping. Bedroom door shut. Finally, he ran out of excuses.

Arnie hunched over the box, a letter opener gleaming in his hand. The illustration from the advertisement haunted the back of his mind. Cartoonish, but so creepy. What if that thing popped out when he slit the tape? Upturned mouth, like a viciously sliced melon rind. Those empty eyes staring at him, hovering in his room.

His safe place.

Stupid, he thought.

Real ghost, his obstinate mind countered.

As he lowered the letter opener, he wondered what Kara Finnegan would think. Would she scream and cower at proof of the afterlife? Perhaps she'd need to be comforted afterward. A stone dropped in Arnie's stomach. The weight of another consideration. What if she looked past the spook, right at Arnie, and what if there was disgust in her eyes? A look of revulsion.

Amaze your friends.

"No," he whispered. He poked the letter opener through the clear tape and the box seemed to groan. A chill of excitement went up his spine, and with his tongue stuck out one side of his mouth, Arnie plunged the knife deeper, pulled it carefully to avoid damaging the contents. The tape split with a sucking sound and the box flaps popped open.

Arnie started to drop the letter opener, then decided against it, squeezing the cool metal tight. Just in case.

Terrify your enemies.

The house seemed entirely too quiet all of a sudden. Any time he was home alone, he heard appliances humming, cars passing, a dog barking down the street. With the package centered on his bed, Arnie heard nothing but the rush of blood in his eardrums. The ocean living in a seashell.

He peered inside.

"Fuck," he muttered, then glanced quickly around as the forbidden word echoed through his room. Hey ho, nobody home.

He reached into the box and pulled out a cheap

cardboard cutout of the specter from the advertisement. Not much larger than a baseball glove and affixed with a string to hang it up.

Arnie blew out a breath. "Cheap Halloween decoration." His throat tightened as he willed himself not to cry. He turned it over, hoping the design at least covered the back as well.

Dull brown cardboard. No design.

Then a flash of red caught his eye. Scribbled beneath the attached string in bright red crayon was a name.

Jonas.

"Seriously? They sent me a used one?"

Arnie thought of the three weeks' allowance he'd blown on this dumb piece of crap, plus the shipping and handling, and the tears came.

Shaking his head, he dropped the ghost back in the box and slammed the flaps as much as it's possible to slam cardboard flaps. He swept the package off the bed and let it *thwump* to the hardwood floor before kicking it under the bed.

With the box out of sight, he collapsed onto his bed, a foot or two above the cardboard spook, and absentmindedly picked at the tiny balls of lint collecting on his pillowcase.

Three days until show and tell, and he needed a

new idea. And it better be a darn good one.

"Something wrong, Arnold?"

His mother spooned a generous helping of garlic-smeared green beans into her mouth and chewed, her eyes resting on him, never wavering. Twig-thin fingers placed her fork down gently, then tented expectantly in front of her plate.

His father never looked up. A folded copy of the Hobson Times lay on the table to the side of his silverware. He chewed like it was labor, peering over the tops of his oversized glasses. Just like the ones Roy Scheider wore in *Jaws*. He'd pretended to read the front page article since the moment he sat down, never bothering to turn the page and lend credibility to the ruse.

Arnie swallowed his bite of dry chicken with a click and grabbed at his glass of water to wash the food down, and buy a little time.

"Everything's great, Mom. No complaints." He faked a smile, then immediately regretted it when his mom frowned.

"You don't look well." She reached across the table

to lay the back of her hand across Arnie's forehead. "No fever. Doesn't he look sickly, Jim?"

Dad grunted and continued pretending to read the paper.

Mom's eyes remained on Arnie, concerned, studying, then her eyebrows shot up. "Say, wasn't your little package supposed to come today? Was it waiting for you when you got home?"

Arnie turned red. Oh, to shrink to the size of an ant and crawl between the floorboards. An ant wouldn't have to search out the words to admit they'd wasted their allowance and chore money on a stupid decoration they could have made with cardboard and some markers. As Mom's smile grew, Arnie's words retreated further inside. She'd told him not to do it, that he was flushing his money down the john. He'd insisted, though, and she even fronted him the stamp, sticking it on the front of the envelope containing the money order with a sing-songy, "Don't say I didn't warn you."

And now he had to come clean. What could be worse than telling a parent they were right, and you were—

CRASH!

All three pairs of eyes flicked toward the ceiling. Even Dad forgot to be uninterested for a moment.

Silence crawled over the supper table. The noise was loud; far from deafening, though. The kind of clatter one could expect if they kept a housecat. Except the McGuire residence kept no pets. Dad's allergies, went the old excuse.

"Arnold," said Mom, her gaze rapt to the ceiling. "That sounded like it came from your room. Is there…"

What? Is there what?

"Something up there we should know about?"

Arnie racked his memory. Had he left something perched on his desk? At the edge of his bed? Finally, he shook his head, his stomach climbing his throat.

"Jim, will you check?"

Dad sighed.

"Jim! What if it's a R-O-B-B-E-R?"

With a second sigh, he rolled his eyes and let them land on Arnie. "The boy can spell, dear." He picked up his napkin from his lap, letting it fall to the table in dramatic fashion, then grumbled and groaned his way up the stairs.

Mom and Arnie sat in silence, listening to Dad's footfalls overhead. They watched the ceiling as if they could keep tabs on him through the wood, carpet, and insulation. The footsteps would move around, and pause. Move and pause. An eternity of stop and go—Mother May I—until the staircase began to creak in all the usual places and Dad returned to the dining room.

Another sigh, like he'd forgotten how to start a sentence without one. "Nothing to report." He plopped into the chair, seizing his fork as he swept his napkin back into his lap. "There was a box in the middle of your floor, Arnie. Might've fallen off your bed."

Arnie nodded, waited for his mother to ask about the Real Ghost again.

"Thanks, Jim," she said, and lowered her eyes to her plate.

Scraping forks and soft chewing filled the air as Arnie's mind raced. He could've sworn he'd kicked the box underneath his bed.

He should've left the light on.

Shadows creeped and swirled as Arnie reached inside the doorframe and felt for the lightswitch, waiting for a cold hand to clamp over his wrist. When his fingers brushed the switch, he flicked it on and remembered to breathe again.

Just as Dad had said, the box lay centered in his room, on display like it should have those red-velvet museum ropes around it. For a moment, Arnie stood framed in the doorway, waiting for the box to move. It refused. Eventually, he would have to enter, find something to do with it.

Don't be stupid. You just left it on the bed and forgot.

Unconvinced, he stepped forward and nudged it with a toe.

Nothing.

Arnie sucked in a breath and dug deep for courage, pictured Kara Finnegan's smiling face, and lifted the flap. There at the bottom of the box was the cartoon spook, staring up at him with those dead eyes, unmoving.

"Jonas," he said, and closed the box again. Then he backed over to his desk, tore a piece of Scotch tape off his dispenser, and applied a hasty seal to the box before pushing it deep underneath the bed and shoving some old clothes around it.

Nothing stirred while Arnie slept. Nothing clattered. When he woke up, the box was still out of sight.

WEDNESDAY

By lunchtime, Arnie had forgotten about the ghost and even managed to push Friday's show and tell to the back of his mind. How could he stress about it with Mickey Willis shoving his face into a plate of mashed potatoes?

"An accident," said Mickey, claiming he tripped over his own feet and happened to brace his fall against Arnie's back. "I really am sorry, Arnie."

"An accident," repeated Mrs. Grinnell, the lunch lady whose voice sounded like the trash compactor from *Star Wars* and smelled like a Marlboro graveyard. "He's sorry. We good here?"

Arnie nodded, and Mickey walked to the other side of the cafeteria to join his friends. The laughter echoing from their table said maybe it wasn't so accidental. Maybe he wasn't so sorry. Even Kara smiled, then reddened and clapped a hand over her mouth when she caught his eye.

"Arnie Mash-Guire," they called, which wasn't very clever, but still managed to sting.

He shoveled a couple more bites, then cleared his tray and went to the bathroom to wash the stray bits of potato flakes from his hair. When he'd washed everything he could down the sink, he looked into the mirror, cheeks red, breathing heavily. Arnie locked eyes with his mirror self.

Mickey Willis stood an inch or two taller than him, wider in the shoulders. Maybe not as fast, though. Arnie closed his fist like his father had shown him, squeezing until his knuckles went white as—

Amaze your friends

—a ghost. One crack to the cheek, better yet the nose, and he could lay Mickey out. Then they wouldn't laugh. Kara wouldn't laugh. The more he thought about it, the more possible it seemed. Speed. Surprise. Then his dad's words came into his head, the ones he'd shared after that afternoon of sparring in the basement.

Don't fight unless you have to. And if it turns out you have to, hit the other guy hard enough to make sure he doesn't get up.

As he stared into the mirror, he could almost see the black and blue bruises forming on his face. He'd never thrown a punch, except at his dad's open palm, and he felt less than confident he could take out Mickey Willis with one punch.

So you're doomed to be known as Arnie Mash-Guire the rest of your life.

Then Arnie had a thought—

Terrify your enemies
—and started working out a plan to match it. He had less than two days.

Upon returning home, part of Arnie believed the box would be in the middle of his room again. He even stood out in the hall and reached inside the cavern that was his room to find the switch, something he'd never done before last night. When the light came on, everything was in its place. Dropping to his stomach, he reached under the bed and pulled the box out. The Scotch tape lay across the flaps like a low-budget burglar alarm.

Nothing in or out.

He set to work while the sun dipped in the sky, interrupted only for a bland dinner with even blander conversation. He wolfed his food down while Mom tried to engage Dad about an item in the paper. *More election crap*, thought Arnie, scraping the last dregs of broccoli off his plate.

"Let's Make America Great Again," read the headline. Dad rolled his eyes, mumbling something about voting for the peanut farmer again.

"May I be excused?" asked Arnie, halfway to the stairs before either of his parents answered.

A length of string. Cut. Another. Strip of tape. A spring. Where can I get a spring? Mechanical pencil, of course. More tape. What about the box? A new one? No. Markers. A lot of markers. Forget the spring. More tape.

Like a mad scientist, he toiled away until Mom's voice pulled him from his obsession.

"Brush teeth," she called up the stairs. "Lights out in five."

There's still more to do. It's not ready.

There's still another day. Tomorrow. Finish tomorrow.

Ten minutes later, he was in bed.

Something pulled Arnie from sleep. A noise? He wet his lips and waited for his eyes to adjust to the darkness, heart beating like a Kiss bassline. All black. No footsteps in the hall. If it was a sound that woke him up, it hadn't stirred Mom or Dad.

Nothing, he thought. *It's nothing.*

He turned to check the time, searching for the

violent green numbers of his alarm clock to tell him how much longer he could sleep. Where his clock usually sat on his bedside table there was only a chasm of—

Don't say it again

—Nothing.

Arnie gulped and heard the sound echo around the small room. "No big deal, no big deal," he whispered to himself. "Power's out, that's all."

Arnold.

A whisper like a cold breeze ruffling his hair.

Then, a flash.

The far side of his bedroom went up in bright light like blowback from a grenade, casting blizzard-white around his room, and no doubt making the blacked-out neighbors wonder if the McGuire house had sucked the power grid dry with some kind of early Christmas light show.

The brightness lasted less than a second in all, blinding Arnie. He blinked four, five times, and welcomed the return of the darkness. Blazing light still hovered before his eyes, but he knew it was a trick. Down to the floating spots in the center. Two dull black eyes, watching. No, not dull.

The eyes were angry. He recognized them. Just not like this.

Help me, Arnold. The same paper-thin whisper of voice.

Arnie screamed until it felt like glass tearing at the inside of his throat.

Footsteps, running. A flood of light from the hall. A voice by his bedside. "What's wrong? What happened?" Genuine care, real concern. And behind all that, a series of green numbers swirling into view.

12:03

"The power," he sputtered. "It's back."

Mom put a hand on his shoulder, rubbing it in small circles, and furrowed her brow. He missed what she said next. The pool of light intruding from the hallway fell on the box in the center of his room, a single flap propped open.

THURSDAY

Mrs. Carey droned on about even numbers versus odd numbers, and try as he might to pay attention, Arnie could barely keep his eyes open. Even the grating screech of chalk against blackboard only offered a temporary reprieve. His head would droop and his eyes would slam shut and a brilliant flash of white took over for the surrounding classroom, always with those dark eyes at the center.

Jonas's eyes.

Then Arnie would snap his eyes open and nod along as if his teacher had just said something exceptionally wise, and he felt compelled to show his agreement.

Nod, zone out, drift off, repeat.

Even the sight of Kara Finnegan, hands clasped on the desk in front of her as she hung on Mrs. Carey's every word, couldn't keep him from sleep. Or Mickey Willis, watching him from the other side of the class with a knowing smirk on his face. One that said, "Let's see what they're serving up in the lunchroom today. A rectangular hunk of pizza."

At least Arnie would know to watch for it today, hopefully avoid another "accident" and another dreadful nickname like "Arnie Mozzarella."

While he tried to keep from drowsing off, he imagined the ghost. He should be scared, terrified even. Had he shoved the box under his bed on Tuesday? He thought so, but he'd been wrong plenty of times before. Last night, though. He was sure, absolutely one-hundred-percent positive he'd closed up the box and tucked it deep underneath his bed.

Either Mom or Dad were playing some awful prank on him, or the ghost—*amaze your friends*—was actually real. And if it worked half as well at show and tell the next day as it worked at home, Mickey—*terrify your enemies*—would be in for an ugly surprise.

"Arnold?"

He snapped to attention.

"Odd or even?"

Kara turned in her seat, looked at him hopefully. Mickey's smirk turned into a full-blown sneer as he mouthed the word, "potato" and lowered his hands to his gut, pretending to laugh.

Not wanting to admit he'd missed the question, Arnie took a stab in the dark.

"It's odd," he said.

Arnie chewed slowly at lunch, barely looking at each bite of pizza, spongy, but with an unpleasant crunch. That didn't matter; he tasted nothing. His eyes roamed like an antelope at a watering hole. The ones from the *National Geographic* video Mrs. Carey had shown during science at the start of the year, where the lanky creatures sipped cautiously at the water until some prehistoric-looking crocodile leapt from the river and clamped its teeth around the antelope's neck. Then it dragged them under, prompting gasps from the class.

Following the video, the first question came from Kara Finnegan. Arnie never would have asked it himself. If a boy asked it, he'd be laughed at, but that didn't keep it from his mind.

"Why didn't the people filming do anything to help?"

Mrs. Carey had paused, looked thoughtful, then smiled like she'd just remembered the practiced answer to the question.

"Because, honey, sometimes you just have to let nature run its course."

That's how it was at Hobson Elementary. Arnie didn't think for a second that old Mrs. Grinnell believed Mickey about the accident the day before. She simply knew her role in the grand scheme of things. To observe and let the crocodile feast.

Arnie stiffened as Mickey walked by, braced against accidental tripping spells, prepared to fight back against something less subtle. Instead, Mickey drifted by, paying no attention. Arnie relaxed and pushed his tray away, no longer hungry.

After lunch, recess. Arnie sat on the tire swing, spinning in circles to match the tempo of his churning stomach while a game of tag went on around him. Yelling, screaming. Gravel kicked up and flew through the air. Arnie breathed in the dust and closed his eyes, thought about what he needed to do at home to finish his project.

Then a flash of light. For nearly a second, Arnie's thoughts turned to the dark eyes from the night before, the ones living in his bedroom. Then a crack of pain erupted in his cheek. He tumbled backward off the tire swing and smacked his head on the loose playground stones.

The bright light gave way to the darkness of closed eyelids. With a groan, Arnie eased his eyes open to find Mickey standing over him with a clenched fist.

"Oops," he said, and ran off to resume the game of tag.

The last touches for his show and tell project came together faster than seemed possible. Like Arnie slipped into a fugue state, the world around him spinning through space like the *Twilight Zone* introduction.

The last bit of string on the spool. Tie it tight. No, double knot. Cut. Punch a hole in the cardboard. Give the string a tug. Holds fast. Perfect. Movement, but not too much. Tongue out, letter the box. Real. Ghost. *Amaze your friends.*

Terrify.

Your.

Enemies.

The high-pitched rip of tape unwinding. Another piece. Another.

Finished?

Finished.

He pushed the box carefully back under the bed.

"Dinner," called Mom up the stairs.

"You want to tell us what happened?" Dad's newspaper lay closed, pushed to the side of his plate. Elbows on the table, he rested his chin on clasped hands.

"I fell off the tire swing." Arnie's voice sounded weak, even to him.

Mom twirled her fork around her plate, her turn to appear uninterested.

"Mmhmm," said Dad. "Looks like you landed on a balled-up fist somebody left laying around. How careless of them."

Arnie searched for a response and came up empty.

"Yes, sir."

Thump!

It came from upstairs. Arnie swallowed, suddenly sure the box would be in the center of his room when he went back upstairs.

"I know a shiner when I see one." Dad smirked. "You hit him back?"

"Jim!" Mom hissed, forgetting to be a fly on the wall.

"No, sir."

"You remember what I told you? About fighting?"

Thump.

Dad raised his eyebrows. "Arnold? Do you?"

"Don't do it unless I have to." Arnie inflected his voice with as much misery as possible.

"That's right," said Dad. "And I hate to be the bearer of bad news, kid, but you're likely in a position where you have to. This other kid. Does he like to pick on people smaller than him?"

Arnie nodded.

Dad raised his head, picked his napkin up off his lap, then dropped it in a crumpled heap on the table.

Thump.

Arnie looked up. "Do you—"

"Bet today wasn't the first time he acted nasty, either. Now that he knows he can get away with something like this, that you won't fight back, he'll do it again."

The words were unpleasant, but Dad's tone sounded encouraging. "So what do I do?" asked Arnie.

Mom frowned and stood, pushing her chair back with a loud scrape, then gathered plates and carried them into the kitchen, while Dad stared at Arnie, studying him.

Thump.

"Show him he's wrong."

Arnie walked into the dark of his room and flipped on the light. Just as he suspected, the box had found its way back to the center of the room. All four flaps stood open and those black, haunting eyes stared up at him. No longer dull.

Gently, Arnie closed his door.

"Jonas," he whispered. "Is your name Jonas?"

No answer.

Arnie swallowed. "I heard you say 'help me' last

night. Let me tell you what I have in mind for tomorrow, then I'll see what I can do to help you."

FRIDAY

When your last name starts with M, you can count on always landing in the middle of every class activity. What great event decided everything in elementary school should occur alphabetically by last name? Arnie couldn't guess. The way it was, the way it always shall be.

With the box shoved down inside a paper grocery bag, Arnie waited for his turn, a warm dampness gathering in his armpits. Lisa Barton went first, showing off a windbreaker she'd gotten for her birthday. A retina-blasting mix of bright pink, purple, and teal.

Jeffrey Carreiro. Emily Clarke. Hannah Darcy.

Boring. Boring. Boring.

Kara Finnegan went next, and Arnie held his breath.

Amaze your friends.

A small green anole with half a mealworm hanging from its mouth stared out from inside of a small plastic critter carrier with a lavender top. Kara called it Aubrey after a TV show about a weird orange lump that did nothing but cause problems. Her face lit up with a big smile while sharing that tidbit, and she received a burst of laughter in return. She looked right at Arnie to see if he joined in, and he flashed a nervous grin, then looked away while she took her seat.

Nathan Garrison. Stephanie Kelly.

Up the alphabet, creeping closer to Arnie.

John McConnell held up a pair of Keds he'd saved for all summer. They were bumblebee black and yellow and appeared fresh out of the store box. With a trace of red in his cheeks, John admitted he was too nervous about scuffing them up to actually wear them. This earned him a polite round of applause.

As John took his seat, Mrs. Carey called Arnie's name.

Cheeks reddening, he considered pretending he'd forgotten all about show and tell. No, that was stupid. Everyone could see the bag next to him. Besides, having nothing for show and tell might prove worse than having something lame.

Here we go, Jonas.

His feet carried him to the front of the room and he cleared his throat. Arnie looked out at all the expectant eyes, finally settling on Kara and offering her a wink.

"Ladies and gentlemen." His voice sputtered, soft. He tried the practiced line again, more bravado this time. "Ladies and gentlemen! I've brought something today the likes of which you've never before laid your fourth grade eyes on."

Eighteen students sat forward, bottoms pulled to the edge of their seats. Arnie put his hand into the paper bag and let it hover there, his arm cut off at the wrist from the audience's perspective.

"Not for the faint of heart. I have brought you today a Real. Live. Ghost."

Several kids gasped, a few laughed. *Amaze your friends.* Mickey Willis groaned and said, "Give me a break."

Arnie smirked. All part of the plan. Carefully, he pulled the box from the paper bag and laid it on the edge of Mrs. Carey's desk to a soundtrack of oohs and ahhs. Even Mrs. Carey seemed intrigued, peering over the top of her glasses. Gone were the shipping label and the dull cardboard-brown of the box. Arnie had painstakingly stenciled REAL GHOST in blood-drip letters from the ad in the *Tomb of Dracula* comic. Small illustrations of the ghost—of Jonas—decorated the rest of the box, and though he'd done a fair job of recreating the gaping eyes and the jagged mouth, it didn't do justice to what lay inside the cardboard prison.

"I need a volunteer to help out, if you'd all like me to show it to you. Real ghosts can be dangerous, so someone has to open the box for me while I prepare to remove it."

Seventeen hands shot into the air. All except for Mickey who crossed his arms over his chest and leaned back in his chair, blowing out a dramatic breath. Even Kara's hand straightened with a slow grace. Any other day and he would've chosen her in a heartbeat, but this wasn't for her.

"How about…" Arnie stroked his chin, pretending to weigh the decision while he waited for Mickey to join the crowd. A spark lit in Mickey's eyes the moment he realized he was alone in his disinterest, and he half-heartedly raised his hand.

"Mickey," called Arnie.

Terrify your enemies.

The boy opened his eyes wide in surprise, then stood unsteadily. In the eight steps from his own desk to the front of the room, Mickey regained his obnoxious swagger, grinning at each student he passed, then beaming at the assembled class while he waited for Arnie to give him his instructions.

"Thanks for the hand. First, we—oh wait." Arnie held up a finger to the class, then reached into the paper bag and pulled out a pair of rubber dishwashing gloves. "Protection," he said, garnering a few nervous laughs. "For me. You should be fine."

Mickey greened. Only a little, but Arnie reveled in it. Gloves on, he picked up the box from the teacher's desk and moved it in front of himself, slow and careful. A show for the audience, as well as a necessary step to ensure the inner workings stayed in place. The loops of string, the makeshift pulleys. If everything went off without a hitch, Arnie suspected Mickey would never bother him or devise another nickname for him again.

Fists aren't the only way to fight back, Dad.

As he turned to present the box to Mickey, Arnie slipped his index finger into the loop of string poking out from the bottom of the box. "Now," he said, "the ghost can be a bit shy, so I'll need you to open the flaps, but move very, very slowly."

Mickey nodded, a bead of sweat collecting on his brow. As he lifted his arms, his hands trembled like David Soul's in *Starsky and Hutch* defusing a bomb in one of the early episodes. As Mickey pulled open one flap—REAL—then the next—GHOST, Arnie tugged at the string, felt the slight resistance, and waited for the spook to burst from the box and scare the daylights out of Mickey Willis.

Every bedroom field test from the previous night had yielded the same results. The cardboard spirit flew from the depths of the box, made to look deeper with a thick layer of midnight black marker. Quick, depending on how hard Arnie pulled the string. He had cut the string to such a length that the ghost would come to an abrupt stop, face to face with the person unlucky enough to open the box. Cardboard it might be, but those eerie eyes and the gaping mouth, drawn to points at the edges, sharp enough to draw blood, would knock any unsuspecting victim on their ass.

Secretly, Arnie hoped the scare might cause Mickey to pee his pants in front of the class.

The ghost emerged, and Arnie felt the resistance of the line hitting its end. Mickey's eyes went golf ball-wide and he stepped back. The ghost kept moving forward, exploding from the box with a frayed piece of string trailing from its backside, still Scotch-taped in place over the name Jonas. It seemed to float in slow motion, a rabid dog attacking an intruder. When it plowed into Mickey's chest, he fell over as if the thing weighed a hundred pounds. He crashed into Emily Clarke's desk, his legs tangling with the desk supports. Boy and desk rolled, clattered to the floor in a ragged heap. Emily screamed.

Shit, shit, oh shit.

Arnie dropped the box and reached for Mickey. Too

late and too far away. He lay in a crumpled pile of flesh and metal with the cardboard ghost on his chest, face out, watching Arnie. Without the advertisement from the comic, without photographic proof, Arnie couldn't swear the ghost's face was different, but he thought it appeared… pleased. The horrifying frown, still turned downward, but less so. The eyes dark and vacuous, but with the illusion of a twinkle.

He hesitated, then lunged forward, snatched the ghost off Mickey's chest. It pulled away like Velcro coming loose, only silent, which was somehow worse, and it felt cold to the touch. Arnie tossed it away, then pushed Emily's desk aside and took Mickey's hand.

The other boy sat up, a dazed look across his face, eyes practically wobbling in their sockets.

"Arnold!" screamed Mrs. Carey. "What a horrible prank to play."

"I'm sorry," said Arnie, quietly. He didn't care if Mrs. Carey heard. Despite the terrible nicknames, the bruises circling his eye, guilt churned in his gut.

I'm not made to fight back, he thought.

When Mickey's eyes focused on Arnie, a smile formed beneath them. No cruelty. It appeared sincere. Arnie tried to remember back to previous grades. Had he ever seen Mickey smile like that before? Genuinely happy?

"...be calling home to your parents," continued Mrs. Carey. "You'd better hope he's alright. John? Go fetch Nurse Doherty and—"

"I'm alright," said Mickey. His voice was measured, calm and soft. "It's okay. I know Arnold didn't mean to hurt me. I just..." His eyes rolled upward like he was searching for a memory. "I got startled and fell over, but I'm not hurt."

Mickey climbed to his feet and brushed his pants off. His eyes wandered again, then lit up. "I haven't been nice to Arnold lately. Maybe for a while. And I guess this makes us even." He held out a hand to shake.

Arnie bit his lip. He'd have to do it with Mrs. Carey watching, but he anticipated a trick, even just a nasty squeeze. When he held out his own hand, Mickey took it, firm but not too hard, and gave it a quick shake.

"Thank you," Mickey whispered, and walked to his desk.

Head spinning, Arnie collected the cardboard ghost, dropped it in the box, and went back to his seat. Mrs. Carey rattled on about show and tell being ruined. As he passed Kara Finnegan, Arnie smiled at her.

Frowning, she lowered her eyes and looked away.

Arnie let himself into the empty house. Mom out running errands and another hour before Dad arrived home to ask if he'd solved his bullying problem. Good. He needed the hour to figure out a way to answer that question.

Up the stairs, into the dark room. Arnie flipped on the light and hung his backpack on his chair, then placed the box on the bed.

Amaze your friends.

His stomach ached even looking at it. Nothing had turned out the way he'd planned. Mickey's actions had been so strange, so out of character, and Arnie couldn't help thinking it was all a charade to lure him into a false sense of security so he wouldn't see it coming when Mickey smashed his face into a gravy-covered lump of potatoes again.

Still, Arnie couldn't shake the change in the other boy.

Terrify your enemies.

Maybe having the tables turned had made Mickey

realize how it felt to be treated like crap. Or maybe Mickey had hit his head after all.

On the bed, the box loomed, casting a shadow across his comforter as the sun lowered in the sky. What to do with the "real ghost?"

He laughed, thinking about all the chores he'd worked to earn the money, the long wait for the package to come in, and his initial disappointment when he'd opened the box.

"Throw it out," he said to no one. The only way to keep it from going bump in the night and trying to escape its under-bed prison.

Sure, he'd made a promise to Jonas, but…

Throw it out.

Arnie nodded in agreement with himself, and picked up the box.

But before you do, a voice whispered. It was different this time, tickling the hair on the back of his neck, *maybe have one more look.*

Against his better judgment, Arnie opened the box. There lay the ghost, staring up. It looked neither angry, nor pleased. Instead, its eyes had a rounded, gleaming quality. Its mouth no longer held a sneer, but a pout.

"It looks scared," he said.

Turn it over.

Turn me over.

Desperate, almost pleading.

Hands trembling, Arnie obeyed the voice, shifting the cardboard between his hands.

It felt cold again.

On the back, string, Scotch tape, and a few hastily scrawled letters, scratched in red crayon.

Mickey, it read.

7. What's to Come
Rob Bilodeau (1990 – 2000's)

Carl settled into his seat in preparation for his first flight. Whereas everyone else on board seemed more nervous, he was anxious to reach their final destination and the adventures that he had planned there. He watched out the window as the ground got further away, laughing to himself about how he was getting away just in time. The flight was going to be a long one, and there wasn't really much to see from above the clouds. Carl decided to get some sleep and let his mind wander, thinking back over his life so far.

He had been named after his great grandfather who immigrated to the United States with his mother in the early days of World War II. They had only intended to stay until the war ended, which they didn't figure would last long. However, when his father had been killed fighting the Allies in the Battle of the Bulge and their home was destroyed, they remained and changed the family name to West. The elder Carl had fought in Korea and his son had fought in Vietnam, so it was no surprise that Carl's father was a Marine. Carl's mother had been killed by a drunk driver on her way home from the grocery store when Carl was in kindergarten, leaving his father to raise him. When his father was deployed to Kuwait as part of Operation Desert Shield, he was sent to live with his mother's older sister and her family in rural Alabama.

The Millers lived in a small three bedroom home, which was rather ordinary looking. It occupied a piece of land at the end of their road which ended in the wood line. The oldest of the Miller children had moved out, leaving just the youngest daughter, Cindy, who was the same age as Carl. As their youngest child, and an unexpected surprise, the Millers doted on Cindy and spoiled her whenever possible.

Carl was expected to help with taking care of the few animals they had, and was only allowed to explore after completing his chores and school work. He enjoyed the quiet of the forest and would slip away to explore any chance he could. It also gave him time to get away from Cindy and her stupid cat, "Whiskers." She would bring that cat everywhere with her, dressing it up in her baby clothes, and insisting that everyone treat it like a person. Carl had never liked cats to begin with, and the fact that he had been forced to leave his dog with the neighbors when he was sent here made him despise the cat all the more. He had to keep reminding himself that his father's deployment would be ending soon and he would be returning home.

His father would write him regularly, and he was always eager to receive news about how things were and what his father was doing. He kept the letters in a small box under the bed and would read them often. Every chance he got to choose what was on the television, he would tune in to the news, hoping to catch his father in the coverage. When Desert Shield became Desert Storm and the US led forces were making quick progress in the war, Carl was sure his father would be home within a couple of months and was anxious for that day. Then, one day when he returned home from school, he saw a strange vehicle in the driveway. Going into the house, he found a couple of soldiers in full uniform and a priest sitting at the table with his aunt. That was when he learned his father had been one of the few Marines who had died in combat, leaving him an orphan at ten.

During that summer was when he decided that he had tolerated Cindy's stupid cat as much as he was going to. He had awoken early to tend to the animals before school and had stepped on a hairball with his barefoot. That was the final straw. It was time for that cat to go. Before anyone else came out, he mixed a little rat poison in with the cat's food. He was careful not to put in too much that it would be noticed. Besides, he didn't want to kill the cat right away; he wanted to make it suffer first. When he returned from school that day, he noticed that the cat had been vomiting and wasn't running around like usual. He even seemed to be withdrawing whenever someone tried petting him. Evidently, his plan was working. But then Cindy threw a tantrum, and it was decided that they would bring Whiskers to see the vet the next afternoon if he hadn't gotten better. That would ruin all of Carl's plans. So the next day, Carl got up a little earlier than usual. He shoved the cat in an old burlap sack and quietly slipped out of the house. Walking into the forest behind the house, he made sure to bounce the sack off of several of the trees, an evil smile creasing his lips each time the cat cried out. He walked to the river that ran through the woods, adding some good sized rocks to the sack as he went, then tied off the top and heaved the sack into the middle of the river. He could hear the cat crying out, and just sat on the shore. Grinning maliciously to himself, he watched the sack sink and heard the cries fade. Then he returned to the yard to tend to the other animals.

When Cindy awoke, he could hear her looking for

her cat. Despite not finding him, her parents had insisted that she go to school and look for him afterwards, sure that he would be there when she returned. He could still recall the look of heartbreak and the sound of Cindy bawling when she remained unable to find her cat after school. He had to concentrate to make sure that he looked as concerned as the adults and avoid any suspicion, but deep down something inside of him reveled in the sensation he had gotten from his actions.

The thrill he got from his first kill improved his mood for a while, but eventually he realized that it was no longer sustaining him. He needed to find some other animal to torture. He began scooping up some of the strays, especially the cats, if no one else was around. He'd bring them to the woods beyond the house to torment and dispose of in the river. And he began to develop different methods of torture for them. One of the methods he was most proud of was when he had glued a stray cat's feet to the road and set its tail on fire. He had barely gotten into the cover of the woods before a passing car had come upon the scene, but by then there was no chance of saving that cat. When he wasn't able to get a stray, he would set traps for some of the smaller animals in the woods and soon realized that he didn't even need to worry about disposing of their bodies. He could just let nature take its course, and nobody would be any wiser.

Throughout this time, Carl continued to grow, and by the time he had turned sixteen, he was taller than the other boys his age. He was able to land a job working after school at the slaughterhouse in town to help with expenses, and found that the work suited him perfectly. As long as he was able to keep up with the demand and the meat wasn't damaged, it seemed like everyone would turn a blind eye if he didn't always follow protocol when he killed an animal. Additionally, the blood on his clothes had become such a common sight that nobody questioned where it had come from.

It was around this time that the excitement he had been getting from killing animals began to decrease, regardless of how often he did it. He needed a new challenge. That was when he noticed the little black girl walking alone down a back road just outside of town. She was probably around eight. Without a second thought, he had struck her in the back of the head with a tree branch and knocked her out. He had taken her into the forest along his walk between work and home and tied her to a tree in an area that he was fairly certain nobody else visited. The excitement he got from her fear was like when he had killed the cat several years prior. For the next few days, he would stop by on his commute and throw rocks at her, until one day he noticed that the animals had finally gotten to her and finished things off. He kept an ear out to hear what anyone was saying about the missing girl, and even after her remains were discovered, people just assumed it was somehow related to the Klan, despite the fact that they hadn't been active in the area for well over a decade.

He knew that he would have to be more cautious about selecting his human victims though, because eventually someone would establish a pattern, and that he would need some sort of shelter in the woods where he could hide them away. Toward that end, he constructed a small shack that he had disguised to look like deadfall. There wasn't much room to stand in the shack, but it was enough to suit his needs. He also started seeking out targets who were less likely to be missed by the police. Drunks were the easiest, but on the rare occurrence that he went to the city, a hooker could be snatched without anyone being any wiser. He would keep them for a few days, inflicting whatever forms of abuse his mind could think up before finally discarding their bodies for the animals to dispose of.

The year he turned eighteen, Carl decided it was time for a new adventure, one which he knew was his life's calling anyway (and the reason he was on this flight). He just had one last detail that he needed to tend to before departing, one that required extra caution.

That was the year that the owner of the slaughterhouse he worked at disappeared, and just a couple of weeks before he was to depart. Carl had been involved in the searches for Ali Khan, like the rest of the town, but the truth of it was he knew exactly where Ali was. How could he not? After all, he was the one who had taken him when he was leaving the office and had him secured in his hidden shack. He had been studying Khan's movements almost since he started at the slaughterhouse, knowing this one would be different and more special than the rest. He wanted to make sure he took a little longer with this one. It was because of towel heads like him that his father had died, and he was going to make Khan pay for all of them.

He could still vividly recall the look of terror on Khan's face when he regained consciousness and realized that he was unable to move. Carl slowly carved a crescent moon into his chest, reminiscent of the stars the Germans made the Jews wear during WWII, enjoying the feeling of his pocketknife pulling and tearing the skin. With all the precautions he had taken building his shack, and previous experience, he knew nobody would hear Khan screaming. Before leaving him alone in the darkness, Carl burned the tips of the fingers on Khan's right hand to ensure that he wouldn't get any ideas of trying to untie his bonds. For the next several days, Carl would visit the shack every chance he could to inflict more pain; some days he would pull a toenail or fingernail with pliers, others he would heat a knife and press it against the flesh until it cooled, then rip it back away, tearing the skin. He would leave a bucket of river water daily and, noticing how quickly Khan was losing weight, forced him to eat some raw entrails that he had taken while he worked.

By the end of the first week, the stench inside the shack was overwhelming, and Khan was noted to have pus oozing from several of his wounds. With only a couple days left before he was to depart, Carl decided it was time to finish the job before Khan just lost consciousness and died in his sleep. That would never suffice. Dragging him out into the depths of the forest, he tied him, fully stretched out, between two trees and disemboweled him. Carl sat drinking a beer as the screams of agony slowly diminished, and he watched the life drain from Khan's eyes. The animals would take care of the carcass. He had wanted to prolong the process, but his greater mission awaited.

The turbulence of their descent woke Carl; they had just arrived in Iraq. It was time to make as many of these rag heads as he could suffer for what he had endured since his father's death, and with the war to hide his activities, he would be free to improve on his torture techniques. A wicked grin creased the corners of Carl's lips as he considered what was to come.

8. My Last Day at Willow Creek High
William Joseph (2000 – 2020's)

Note from the author:

Trigger Warnings: This story is full of extreme graphic elements related to sensitive topics such as school shootings. Please be warned.
While this is a work of fiction, if you or a loved one need mental health help, services, or intervention, please contact your local Emergency Hotlines, or dial 988 for the Suicide & Crisis Hotline, which is available 24/7. And if you ever suspect someone is going to harm others, or see a threat online, please contact your local authorities *immediately*.
If you see something, say something.
We're all in this together.

To victims of gun violence.
I will never stop speaking up for you.

November 17th, 2025

The morning sun filtered through the cracked windows of Willow Creek High, spilling an unsettling, golden haze that danced upon the dust motes, swirling like trapped spirits in a forgotten tomb. As the homeroom bell rang, the students cascaded through the building's dim halls, but beneath their laughter and chatter, a sinister heaviness clung to the air, thick as a shroud.

Only Mary, the quiet girl in art class, felt the oppressive weight of wrongness in the atmosphere. She was never like the others; her senses were tuned to the whispering shadows, perceiving the ghostly creaks of the aged wooden floorboards and the flickering overhead lights. She noticed the things nobody else paid any attention to or gave much thought. Even the snide remarks of her peers, shrouded in triviality, slithered around her like whispers from the grave—she barely acknowledged them, their venomous words lost within the noise of her thoughts.

Mary sat at her easel, headphones clamped tight

against her ears, absorbed in the creation of her senior project. It was an oil painting, but not just any painting—it was the embodiment of Fear itself. Her teacher, Mrs. Fischer, relished in tormenting her students for the sake of progress and art, relentlessly pushing them toward some lofty ideal of artistry.

"Art, without meaning, isn't art," she would declare, her voice resonating with an otherworldly authority. Each stroke of the brush had to reflect a dark truth, a struggle forged from the depths of one's soul. Failing to adhere to such demands was a fate worse than poor grades; it was a death knell for their aspirations. Those who emerged victorious from her grasp could earn an art scholarship, a golden ticket to Willow Creek University for Art and Design.

At first, the dread Mary was feeling was merely an inkling, a nagging sensation gnawing at the edges of her consciousness. She dismissed it as typical teenage paranoia, but deep down, a primal terror clawed at her gut, whispering of a darkness that stirred, waiting. She couldn't fathom why, but whatever it was lingered just out of sight, insatiable, seeping into the cracks of her world and threatening to consume her whole.

Mary gazed intently at her painting, the

brushstrokes capturing the very essence of fear. What did that word evoke in her? It stretched beyond the mere fright of a spider lurking in a corner or the spindly legs of a cricket chirping in the dark. It transcended the heartbreak of loss or the gnawing pain of a loved one's departure. To Mary, fear was desolation itself—a harrowing abyss of solitude that enveloped her, crushing her spirit as she stood silent against adversity.

Her mind drifted back to the moment that fear materialized with the chilling clarity of a distant echo—the class trip to the city during her elementary years. What began as an adventure of wonder and awe soon spiraled into a nightmare. The shrieking beauty of the art museum, with its majestic galleries and haunting pieces, had ignited a spark of inspiration within her. She documented everything in her journal—from the impossibly tall skyscrapers and the chaotic graffiti pulsing with life, to the jarring reality of the homeless. Each moment, a testament to the vibrant, yet terrifying heartbeat of the city.

But it was the journey back home that shattered her innocence.

The bus ride home became a dark descent into horror when a drunk driver barreled into them, shattering their fragile world. In her mind's eye, she replayed the chaos—the screech of tires on asphalt, the shattering glass, the screams piercing the air like mourning crows as the bus turned on its side and everyone was thrown from their seats in a violent but swift jerk. The aftermath unfolded like a grotesque painting: the death of a chaperone, a teacher, and two of her classmates splashed across a canvas of tragedy. In the sterile hospital room, she could almost feel the sharp sting as they removed shards of glass from her arm, leaving behind faint scars that glimmered even today in the right light—a constant reminder of that harrowing day when Fear transformed from an abstract concept into an agonizing reality.

The shrill sound of the bell jolted Mary from her mental prison, cutting through her dark thoughts like a blade. It signaled the end of the first period, thrusting her back into the thrumming heart of Willow Creek High. With dread pooling in her stomach, she prepared herself for the crowds that awaited her in the halls. Stowing her art supplies, she slung her bag over her shoulder, a lifeline tethering her to the mundane.

Navigating through the sea of blank faces, each a ghostly blur merging into one another, she fished her phone from her pocket and changed the song, seeking solace in the sound. The screech of laughter, the murmur of voices felt like a haunting chorus that prickled her skin. After English, the cycle repeated, but this time she ventured into the History wing, then toward Math.

As she stood at the convergence of two halls, intent on altering the music yet again, an unseen force yanked her from her own world. She stumbled, her heart racing as the icy grip of her phobia tightened around her throat, and for a fleeting moment, the hall seemed to close in, the faces of her classmates contorting into monstrous visages. Panic flickered in the corners of her mind, but she fought against it, desperately grasping for balance.

"Asshole," she spat out, the word lost in the thunderous roar of the music that crashed over her like wild waves.

Eminem's "Rap God" jolted through her ears, drowning out everything around her, but the tide of bodies relentlessly surged, each unyielding shove against her becoming more vicious, more unforgiving. Then she collided with someone and they both tumbled to the cold, lifeless tile.

Her face hovered inches from the ground, the chill seeping into her skin, a stark contrast to the chaos echoing in her mind. Panic surged through Mary as she wondered if this was it—was she being jumped in a fight she hadn't even realized that she had started?

As she struggled to regain her bearings, her gaze fell upon her phone, a mere yard away, but it was the sight beyond it that twisted her stomach into knots. The student who had knocked her over was wide-eyed, staring at her with a horror that sent icy tendrils of fear crawling up her spine. His finger jabbed into the chaotic throng behind her, mouth moving furiously, though amidst the beat of the music, his frenzied shouts faded into unheard muffles.

With a pounding heart, Mary yanked one of her AirPods free.

"Run!" His voice erupted, thick with terror. "He's got a gun!"

The words hit her like a heavy blow but hung, ungrasped, in the air. For a split second, she felt a dissonance between his command and reality. Mary was paralyzed, rooted to the stark tile as the pandemonium swarmed around her, until she finally turned to see what had ignited such panic.

Dozens of students surged in all directions as chaos enveloped the hall. But amongst them, moving deliberately and unnaturally slower, was a figure that carved a path through the stampede.

He was tall and slender with long black hair slicked back, revealing a face unmarred yet adorned with acne scars that seemed to soak in the dread that loomed. Clad in an unsettling combination of black and forest-green camouflage, the air around him felt thick, suffocating.

In his hands, he cradled what looked like an automatic rifle, its sinister appearance whispering unspeakable intentions. Even without the knowledge of firearms, Mary recognized the predator amongst prey—a palpable threat that radiated dread and danger, swallowing her hope whole. Time screeched to a halt as a primal instinct surged within her: survival.

The boy, a stranger with hollow, lifeless eyes, raised his weapon with a calculated calm that made Mary's stomach churn. Without hesitation, he opened fire on the students scattered between him and Mary. The sharp crack of the gun echoed down the hallway. A boy's calf burst open in a violent spray of blood and muscle, sending him crumpling to the ground. His agonized screams pierced the chaos before a pair of trembling hands yanked him into a classroom, the floor smeared in his blood, the door slamming shut with a finality that seemed to seal his fate.

A girl—her face vaguely familiar but now a mask of terror—was struck next. She had been running, her sneakers skidding on the polished floor slickened with blood. She stumbled, arms flailing, before hitting the ground. She clawed at the floor, desperate to escape, but the shooter was already there, towering over her. His heavy black boot crashed down onto her backpack, pinning her to the floor.

She whimpered, her eyes met Mary's, then tears streaked her face as he aimed the weapon at her head. "Please," she begged, her voice cracking, but her pleas were swallowed by the cold, mechanical click of the trigger.

The shot shattered the air—and her head. A gruesome explosion of flesh, bone, and brain matter splattered across the floor, painting it in a macabre display. Her body twitched once, then fell unnervingly still, her final expression a ghastly look of terror.

Mary flinched violently, her entire body trembling as the coppery scent of blood filled her nose. Her heartbeat thundered in her ears, her breath shallow and frantic. She hadn't even realized she had been holding her breath until it left her in a ragged gasp.

Suddenly, hands gripped her from behind, rough

and urgent, and yanked her to her feet. She spun around, startled, to see the boy who knocked into her—his face pale and streaked with sweat—pulling her toward him.

"Move!" he barked, his voice raw and panicked.

Behind them, the shooter turned his attention to another classroom. The screams of students trapped inside erupted as the door splintered under the force of his kick. Shots rang out, each one punctuated by a deafening silence that followed.

Mary's legs felt like lead, but the boy's grip was unyielding, dragging her down the hallway. The corridor seemed endless, lined with history classrooms now filled with cowering, doomed students. Her vision blurred, every sound amplified—the distant wails, the wet thuds of bodies hitting the floor, the ceaseless, unrelenting shots.

"Don't look back," the boy growled, his voice shaking as they sprinted forward. Mary didn't need to. The horrors she'd seen already were seared into her mind, playing on an endless, nightmarish loop.

Mary's legs burned as she sprinted, her sneakers slipping on the floor. The boy pulling her along had a death grip on her wrist, his breathing as rapid as hers. The sounds of chaos behind them—a mix of screams, shattered glass, and gunfire—faded slightly as they turned the corner into the other history wing. For a moment, the hallway was eerily quiet, the silence thick and oppressive.

"Keep moving," the boy encouraged, barely sparing her a glance.

The fluorescent lights above flickered erratically, casting long, distorted shadows on the walls. Mary's mind raced, her thoughts a jumbled mess of fear and disbelief. The boy's hand was clammy against hers, and she could feel the tremor in his grip.

They passed several classrooms, their doors shut tight. Some had desks barricaded against them, others were eerily open, their interiors dark and still.

Suddenly, a sound—a faint metallic click—echoed down the hall. Mary froze, her heart lurching painfully in her chest. The boy stopped too, his head snapping toward the sound.

From the far end of the hallway, two figures emerged. They moved with a chilling confidence, their boots thudding heavily against the tile. Both carried weapons, larger and deadlier than the one wielded by the first shooter. The taller of the two wore a black hoodie smeared with crimson streaks, the other a pale mask that gleamed under the flickering lights.

The one in the mask spotted them first, his head tilting unnaturally to the side, as if appraising his prey. Without a word, he raised his weapon.

"Run!" the boy screamed, shoving Mary forward as the first shot cracked through the air.

Mary ducked instinctively, the bullet whizzing past her ear and slamming into a locker behind her. The metallic clang reverberated down the corridor. She bolted, her breath coming in short, panicked gasps. The boy was right behind her, his footsteps pounding frantically against the floor.

They veered into one of the open classrooms, slamming the door behind them. The boy scrambled to push a desk in front of it, his hands shaking so badly he nearly dropped it.

"Help me!" he begged, his voice laced with desperation.

Mary grabbed another desk, her fingers slick with sweat and trembling so violently that she struggled to get a grip on it. They stacked it against the door just as the shooters reached it. A loud bang echoed through the room as one of them slammed against the door, testing the makeshift barricade.

"Little pigs, little pigs," a voice cooed from the other side, mockingly. It was the one in the mask. "Let us in."

The other shooter laughed, a low, guttural sound that sent a chill racing down Mary's spine.

The boy grabbed her arm, pulling her toward the back of the room where a supply closet stood. "In there," he whispered harshly.

Mary hesitated, her eyes darting between the closet and the door, which now rattled violently as the shooters tried to force it open. Another gunshot rang out, splinters flying from the wood as a bullet punched through the door.

"Go!" he snapped, shoving her toward the closet.

They squeezed inside, the cramped space reeking of stale air and old cleaning supplies. The boy eased the door shut, leaving it open just a crack.

Mary could see through the narrow slit, her view fixed on the classroom door.

The pounding stopped. Silence fell, thick and suffocating. Mary held her breath, her pulse thundering in her ears.

A faint scrape broke the quiet—a blade, dragging lazily along the doorframe.

Then, a whisper. "We know you're in there."

The classroom door creaked open, the barricade shoved aside effortlessly. The boy covered Mary's mouth with his hand, his own breath hitching as the two shooters stepped into the room.

Through the crack in the closet door, Mary saw them. The one in the hoodie walked slowly, his weapon trained on every shadow. The masked one trailed behind, dragging a long, gleaming knife across the desks.

They were toying with them, savoring the hunt.

Mary clenched her fists, her nails biting into her palms. She wanted to scream, to cry, to do anything but sit there helplessly as the shooters prowled closer.

The boy leaned in, his lips brushing her ear. "If they find us, we run. Don't stop. Don't look back."

Mary nodded, though her legs felt like jelly.

The masked shooter suddenly stopped, his head snapping toward the closet.

Mary's heart plummeted.

The shooter tilted his head again, then reached for the closet door.

The closet door began to creak open, revealing the masked shooter's ghastly visage. His eyes, dark and void of humanity, met Mary's. She wanted to scream, but her throat locked tight. She couldn't move, couldn't breathe.

The boy beside her didn't hesitate. With a desperate yell, he slammed the door into the shooter's face, sending him stumbling back. Before

Mary could process what was happening, the boy lunged out of the closet, tackling the second shooter with feral intensity.

"Go!" he bellowed, his voice raw.

Mary's legs finally obeyed, and she bolted from the classroom, tears streaming down her face. Just as she cleared the doorframe, a deafening gunshot echoed behind her. A bullet struck the wall inches from her head, spraying her with shards of plaster. She stumbled, nearly losing her balance, but kept running.

Then she heard it—the boy's scream.

She froze, her body trembling as another gunshot rang out. The sound seemed to pierce her soul. Her vision blurred, but she forced herself to move, her only thought to get away.

The hallway was a maze of carnage. She slipped on a slick patch of blood, hitting the floor hard. Pain flared in her palms as they met the unforgiving tile. Gasping, she looked down, noticing the thick, sticky liquid pooling around her hands.

But it wasn't just pooling—it was moving.

The blood, dark and glistening, slithered across the floor like a living thing. It pulled itself together from the scattered puddles nearby, the crimson streamlines merging into a single, growing mass.

Mary's breath caught as she noticed the bodies lying nearby. Their faces, twisted in unnatural expressions of terror, seemed to be watching the blood's grotesque transformation.

The mass began to rise, stretching and twisting until it formed a horrifying shape that was like an extracted human vascular system, pulsating and throbbing as though it had a heartbeat of its own. Veins and arteries connected and pulsed, but there was no flesh, and no body to contain it.

Mary scrambled backward, her shoes squeaking against the floor. She pressed herself into the corner, shaking violently.

The shooters then emerged and stepped out of the classroom she had fled from. They froze at the sight of the blood-formed monstrosity.

"What the hell is that?" the masked one muttered, his voice trembling.

"It's not real," the other snapped, though his words lacked conviction.

The masked shooter stepped closer, raising his weapon cautiously. He fired a shot, the echo reverberating down the hallway. Mary flinched, but the bullets didn't harm the thing. Instead, it shuddered slightly, splattering droplets of blood on the walls and floor where the bullet had passed through.

"See? Nothing," the shooter said as he approached it.

Then he reached out.

The moment his gloved hand touched the blood, it sprang to life. Tendrils of crimson lashed out, wrapping around his arm. He screamed, a high-pitched, animalistic wail, as the thing snapped his arm in half, the bone instantly protruding. Then it pulled him closer. In an instant, the tendrils went under his clothes and pierced his body, tearing through flesh and bone with sickening ease.

Mary watched in abject horror as the shooter was shredded into a spray of gore, his remains splattering across the walls and floor. The other shooter fired wildly, his shots tearing through the air but doing nothing to the monstrous entity.

Before he could flee, the blood creature surged forward. It grabbed him, tendrils wrapping around his torso. He shrieked, his body convulsing as the thing wrenched him apart with a grotesque, wet snap. Blood and viscera painted the hallway in a macabre display as his torso and legs went in opposite directions.

Mary was frozen, her body numb as the creature turned toward her. Its pulsing form radiated a chilling intelligence, as though it somehow recognized her.

The distant wail of sirens reached her ears, but she couldn't move. The thing began to advance, its bloodied silhouette leaving streaks on the floor.

Suddenly, as she turned the corner to flee, a figure stepped in front of her and blocked the hallway. It was the last shooter.

"Get down!" he barked.

Mary dropped to the floor as he pointed his gun at her. Then, a loud wet sound rang out, and the bloody creature appeared in the center of the intersecting halls. The shooter aimed at the blood creature, unloading his clip in a frantic barrage. The bullets did nothing. The thing surged forward, enveloping him in seconds.

The shooter's screams were short-lived. The blood creature crushed him, leaving behind a mutilated heap of flesh and bone within.

Mary's body trembled violently as the thing turned its attention back to her.

Its form shifted, a grotesque mimicry of a human shape. It loomed over her, its bloody vein-like tendrils twitching.

The hallway doors then burst open, and the police stormed in. The creature froze, its pulsating mass quivering. Then, as though sensing their presence, it collapsed.

The blood splashed to the floor, covering Mary and the surrounding walls in a thick, crimson coating.

"Hands up!" one of the officers shouted, his weapon trained on her.

Mary didn't move, her body paralyzed with shock.

The officers rushed to her, pulled her to her feet, and guided her toward the exit. The chaos of the last hour seemed to melt away as she stepped outside into the cold, fresh air.

Mary never returned to the school. The building remained closed for the rest of the year, a grim monument to the horrors within. She finished her senior year at home, haunted by the memories of that day—and by the bloodied, inhuman silhouette that had either spared her, or saved her.

She still wasn't sure which.

9. The Beating Heart of Colony Three
Timothy King (3000's)

"What's the word, Cap?" Miguel Perez asked. He put his helmet on, leaving the faceplate dangling to the side. Jogging to catch up, he fell into step with his Captain.

"It's the damn Mormons again," Captain Jerome Brown muttered.

"Of fucking course it is."

The air outside was humid, even for the summer on Colony Three. It was an ugly planet. Gray shale-like rocks coated every inch of the surface. Its vast open terrain was treeless, save for a few slender vines that snaked up through the rock. Thick dust particles rolled through the sky, giving the illusion of monstrous clouds and painting the sky with a blood-red hue.

They rounded a corner and emerged onto a concrete slab where three other men awaited them. The men stood in a single line, milling about and talking excitedly. Metal packs stood upright on the ground before them, their rifles resting neatly against them.

It was precisely as Captain Brown had trained them. As he approached, one of the men called the squad to attention. The three men snapped their heels together, with their hands down at their sides.

Stopping a few feet in front of his men, Jerome put his hands behind his back. "Alright, listen up." He turned and walked a few steps to his right. "Against the advice of the colonial committee, a fringe group of Mormon extremists set up a base outside of the green zone." He did a quick about-face and marched back across the row of men. "As of two weeks ago, they stopped responding to transmissions." Jerome stopped pacing and turned in front of his men. Shifting his weight, he continued. "We have been tasked with investigating the cause for their lack of communication."

One of the men opened his mouth to speak but stopped when Captain Brown held out a hand. "I know. I know," he said, shaking his head. "It's probably a malfunction with their communication equipment." He cracked a wry smile. "Mormons aren't exactly known for their technological capabilities." This earned a subdued chuckle from his men. "Still," he continued, "we will treat this as a hostile mission until it's proven that it isn't." The men nodded their heads subtly.

Holding up a finger, Jerome spun it in the air, motioning to the hopper on the launch pad behind his men. The metal bird roared to life. A blast of hot air rippled past the men as their ride's jet engines whined. "Sergeant," he said, looking at Miguel. "Move 'em out."

Miguel stepped forward, seamlessly transitioning into his leadership role. "Alright, ladies! You heard the man. Grab your shit and get on the bird." He took a few steps towards their ride, waving his men on. "Come on, you apes! You wanna live forever?"

In a nearly synchronized movement, the three soldiers dipped down and grabbed their packs. They swung the bags over their shoulders, stood up, and draped their rifles across their chest. Without speaking, they turned around and jogged toward the hopper.

Sergeant Perez nodded to his Captain then took off after the men.

Jerome smiled to himself. Miguel had really whipped these men into shape. With his own recent promotion to captain, he would need to find a new lieutenant. He followed his men at a brisk pace, wondering if the Colonial Commander would sign off on an in-field commission for his reliable NCO.

Jerome decided he would broach the subject with the commander after this mission. In his mind, Miguel had earned it.

He reached the hopper, ducking under its wings. Hot air broiled from the jet engines, nearly singeing his eyebrows. Jerome quickly snapped his facemask into place. The tactical HUD in his visor blinked to life as soon as the clasp was secure. It always took about two seconds for the suit to pressurize and for oxygen to flow into his helmet. He hated those two seconds. To him, it always felt like he was sealing his own coffin. In many ways, he was. If he died on a mission in the colony worlds, it would be unlikely anyone would expend the resources to recover his body, at least until they were ready to build on the spot where his corpse rested.

The men piled into the bird, taking their positions along a bench seat. They left the bucket seat across from them open for their Captain. He reached out and grabbed a handrail, pulling himself into the belly of the craft. Dropping into his seat, he nodded to his men. The emotionless expressions of their facemasks stared back at him. His eyes filtered across them. Victor's mask was painted red, an homage to his home on Mars. It made Jerome think of his own home on Titan, a place he hadn't seen in nearly ten years.

Shaking away the thought, he held up his forearm, allowing him to see the screen built into his suit. He opened a communication channel with the pilots. "Let's go."

Without a response, the jet engines tilted down, flooding the cabin with hot air. A warning light flashed in his HUD, indicating a sudden change in temperature. He dismissed it without concern.

They wouldn't even notice the shift from within their suits.

The jet shuddered as the engines spewed fire. It rose ever so slightly and lingered a few inches off the ground. Jerome felt a knot form in his stomach as their ride spun in a three hundred sixty-degree turn and lurched into the sky. They soared into the air at incredible speeds, causing his suit's alarm to go off with an altitude warning. The atmosphere of Colony Three was incredibly similar to Earth's, with only one exception. Colony Three's atmosphere turned into almost pure carbon dioxide after a few thousand feet.

Jerome leaned back in his seat and clenched his eyes shut. He was thankful that his mask obscured his face from his team. The abrupt takeoff of the Vertibirds always made him feel sick. Taking a deep breath of his suit's recycled oxygen, he stifled the urge to vomit.

After a few more moments of rapid climbing, the engines rotated to angle their flames towards the rear. The aircraft lurched forward, accelerating toward the sunset of their dual stars at breakneck speed.

A yellow light flashed in the center of the cabin. "This is your captain speaking." The voice came over the intercom in their helmets. "Today's flight will be approximately twenty minutes. We expect clear skies and little turbulence on the way to Fort Joseph Smith." There was a pause in the pilot's cadence and the jet veered slightly to the right. "I must remind you to keep your head and hands inside the vehicle at all times." Another pause and the aircraft leveled out. "This is a non-smoking Vertibird. Thank you for flying with us here on Colony Three."

Jerome looked around to see his men shaking their heads. Perez's name appeared in the corner of his display in green with a speaker icon.

"Do they ever get tired of that lame-ass joke?" he said into the squad communication channel.

Another icon popped up next to Miguel's, signaling that their newest private, Killian Patrick, was attempting to break into the channel. Jerome sighed and used the eye-tracking software to allow the kid to speak.

"I thought it was really funny!" Killian exclaimed as soon as he came on the net.

"That's because it's the first time you've heard it, boot. Tell me if that shit is still funny after your fortieth mission," Corporal John Myers grunted.

"Have you really been on forty missions?" Killian asked incredulously.

Myers nodded. "Today is number forty." He pointed to Captain Brown. "Hell, I've run twenty-three of them with the boss."

"Too bad twenty of them turned out to be nothing but lost colonists and wild animals," Captain Brown snickered.

Myers laughed. "Yeah, but those other three were pretty wild."

Killian smacked Myers in the arm. "Can you tell me about them when we get back to base?" he asked. His eagerness made him sound like a child asking to open his Christmas presents a day early.

"Yeah, kid. I'll tell you all about them when we get back."

Perez's icon appeared in Jerome's hud. "Yeah, but you're buying the beer."

The pilot's call sign broke through the

communication channel, overriding the small talk. "Five minutes till touch down!" he called out.

Jerome held up five fingers, signaling to his men to prepare. He hated this part almost as much as takeoff. Any minute now, the Vertibird would plummet toward the ground in a vicious nosedive. The men would be thrust into their seats from the G-force, forcing them to fight the urge to pass out. Despite all of the missions he had been on in his career, the flying never got any easier for him.

Jerome grimaced as the nose of the aircraft tilted down. A loud whistling sound rang out from the wind rushing past the aircraft as it dove. An alert went off in the corner of Jerome's display, indicating an increase in G-force. It climbed to nine Gs. Under normal circumstances, the men would begin blacking out under this much pressure. Luckily for them, their suits helped maintain even blood flow. They continued their descent for a few more seconds before the aircraft leveled out violently. The sudden change in momentum jerked the men around. Jerome could hear several of them moaning in discomfort. Without warning, the bird came to a stop. It hovered about a foot off the ground. A green light filled the cabin, and without a second thought, Perez leapt from the aircraft.

Jerome watched the men file out of the bird. They fanned out in all directions, dropping to a knee with their rifles raised. It was just as Jerome had trained them. Once all of the men were out of the Vertibird, Jerome jumped out of the cabin.

"Clear. Clear. Clear," he called over the squad net.

The soldiers rushed forward, expanding their perimeter around the aircraft to one hundred meters per army doctrine. Once they were clear of the blast area, the Vertibird's engines roared back to life. They flooded the landing zone with superheated exhaust as it rocketed back into the sky. Within seconds, the aircraft had disappeared into the rolling clouds above.

Sergeant Perez looked over his shoulder at Captain Brown. When Brown nodded, he sprung into action. Leaping to his feet, he tapped two men on the shoulder as he rushed past them. The two men immediately jumped to their feet and sprinted after their sergeant.

Captain Brown paused to take in his surroundings. A few hundred yards away stood a metal fortress. The massive building rested on a series of support columns, which lifted the entire structure off the ground. A long ramp protruded from the front of the building. It rose off the ground, leading to two iron doors that looked like they could withstand an atomic blast.

Brown knew it was the headquarters of the Mormon mission on Colony Three. The religion had grown exponentially in the past few years, setting up missions on every colony planet. They were known for branching out on their own, building their bases far from the prying eyes of the government or the corporations.

"Cap, we're in position." Perez's voice rang out through his radio. Shifting his eyes from the large building to a series of rocky outcroppings to the left, he saw his three men kneeling in a defensive posture with their weapons pointing in different directions.

"Let's move," Brown bellowed out over the squad channel. In unison, he and Killian sprinted toward the group.

Captain Brown slid into position next to the Sergeant.

Anticipating his Captain's next order, Perez's voice broke through the radio. "Myers, take Killian and see if anyone is home."

Wordlessly, Myers jumped to his feet and sprinted toward the enormous ramp. After about twenty-five yards, he paused and looked back.

Killian was still squatted in his position, scanning

the desolate landscape around them.

Perez grabbed the kid by the shoulder and gave him a violent shake.

Killian whirled around to face his Sergeant, who immediately flicked his visor and pointed toward Myers.

"Shit," Killian said into the open channel. "Sorry, Sarge."

"Just move your ass," Perez replied with an exasperated sigh. Killian spun on his heels and sprinted toward Myers. Together, the two men jogged up the ramp to the massive building.

When they reached the top, Killian moved to the left, holding his rifle at the ready. Myers reached the speaker system on the side of the gate and pressed the communication button. Nothing happened. He pressed it again and listened for a response from someone in the fortress.

He looked down at the three men still on the ground. Shaking his head, he radioed the squad. "No joy."

Jerome sighed. He pointed toward the third man in the squad. "Henry, get up there and make entry."

"Yes, Sir," The soldier responded. He jumped to his feet and sprinted up the ramp toward the door.

Captain Brown and Sergeant Perez stood up and

jogged toward the ramp.

Private Victor Henry reached the massive double doors and slung his rifle over his shoulder. Digging through his pocket, he produced a small metallic tube about the size of a pen. He pressed it against the door and clicked a button on the back. A red light emitted from the end of the tube. Within seconds, the laser was eating through the metal door. Flames flashed and extinguished as he moved the laser around the door, creating a rectangle large enough for the men to fit through. When he finished, he returned the laser to his pocket. Taking a step back, he kicked the cut-out piece of metal.

A large chunk of the metal door collapsed inward. It fell to the ground with a loud, clang that echoed off the walls of the building.

Henry stepped back and allowed Killian and Myers to enter the building first. They worked in well-practiced unison, sweeping the room of threats. Henry walked into the building after them, his rifle held high.

Jerome and Perez reached the entry a few seconds later and pushed through the opening.

Jerome expected to see the Mormons gathering around to confront the intruders, but there was nobody around. They found themselves in a massive atrium that stretched hundreds of feet above them. A picture of what Jerome assumed to be the Mormon god was painted overhead, his eyes seeming to track the intruders in his sanctuary.

Wordlessly, the men worked their way through Fort Joseph Smith. They took it slow, clearing the building hallway by hallway and room by room.

Jerome expected to see a Mormon colonist every time they turned a corner. He was sure they would emerge from the shadows and explain what happened here. Racking his brain, he tried to imagine what could be causing their absence. The building was pristine. There were no signs of struggle. No blood or bullet holes adorned the walls. He went through scenarios in his head.

Life support failure? He scrolled through his interface until he found the atmospheric scanner. Activating it, a yellow light flashed in the corner of his hud then turned green, indicating the air was safe to breathe. Jerome shook his head.

The men rounded a corner into another of the building's endless hallways with Myers in the lead. He took a few steps then held up a closed fist. The group came to a stop and dropped to a knee. They scanned the area with their rifles.

"Captain, I hear a buzzing noise coming from the

end of this hallway."

Jerome sighed in relief. They'd finally have some answers and could return to base. "Push on," he ordered. "We have to figure out what happened to the Mormons."

Myers stood back up and led the team down the hallway. The buzzing sound grew louder as they walked. It morphed from a low hum that reminded Jerome of construction machinery, to a high-pitched crackle of static.

They reached a turn in the hallway and stacked up along the wall. Myers waited for everyone to fall into position, then, with his rifle up, turned the corner.

The scene before him nearly shattered his psyche. It came to him in frozen images, fitting together like a jigsaw puzzle. His rifle fell to his side. "What the fuck?" he whispered.

The others appeared at his side, all equally dumbfounded.

The hallway opened into another large atrium, but unlike the entryway, this one was overgrown with enormous red vines. They clung to every surface. A thick canopy dangled from the ceiling. Thick veiny lines carved a path across the vines. They pulsated with a steady rhythm. Their pointed tips wiggled like worms trying to slither their way toward the soldiers.

And then there were the bodies.

Men, women, and children, all dressed in the white robes of the Mormon mission, lay lifeless within the mess of vines. They constricted and loosened repeatedly, squeezing the fluids from the decaying bodies. A few of the corpses even had vines running through them. They had punched out of chest cavities and stomachs like in the ancient Alien movies.

"I've seen these vines before," Perez muttered. He took a cautious step forward. "There's a bunch of them growing by the base." He approached one of the pulsating vines. Its pointy end wriggled on the floor as if seeking out its prey. "I've never seen them move, though."

"Don't get too close," Jerome ordered. "I gotta call this in." He looked around, trying to take in as much of the scene as possible. The camera in his helmet would record everything, and he could include it in his after-action report. Toggling through channels, he spoke to the base. "Spartan One to Spartan Actual. Over." When no reply came, he tried again. "Spartan Actual, this is Spartan One. Over." His heartbeat quickened. He'd heard of ancient militaries having communications issues, but in his nearly twenty years of service, he'd never experienced it for himself.

Turning back to his men, Jerome motioned with his hand for the men to move forward. "I can't reach base. Let's push on and see what we can find."

The rest of the men entered the room. They slowly worked their way across the atrium toward a flashing sign that read, "The Prophet's heart." The men moved carefully, stepping over the pulsating vines and avoiding the bodies as they swayed in the sea of red. They maintained their formation throughout all of the horrors, their extensive training guiding them.

Ahead of them, Jerome could see a hole in the ground. He expected to see a mass of wriggling vines stretching out from the darkness, but none of the vines came anywhere near it. The men formed a semicircle around the opening and peered down.

The beams of the fluorescent lights above them only managed to illuminate the first few feet of the hole, revealing rock walls.

Perez forced himself to peel his eyes from the opening in the ground to face his Captain. "Did they dig this?" he asked, using a private channel.

"It looks like it," Jerome answered. He unzipped the pouch he kept fastened at his hip and pulled out a small white tube. Twisting the top, the flare ignited. Streaks of bright red flames exploded from the end, bathing the room in an unnatural red tone. The visor in his helmet clicked as it automatically tinted itself to protect his eyes. Holding it over the hole, he hesitated. Something deep inside his core told him not to drop it. They could turn around and signal for a lift. Command might even blow the entire building up if they thought these vines were a threat. Then he thought about the vines growing around the colony and realized he had to go down there.

He dropped the flare and watched it plummet into the hole.

It fell far longer than Jerome had expected it to, its flame battling against the oppressive darkness. At the edges of its light, Jerome swore he saw movement. He shook his head. The flare landed on a pile of rocks a few hundred feet below them.

Waving his fingers, he motioned for his men to move into the hole. They worked in the kind of silence only trained men can manage. Each man secured himself to a rappelling rope, then secured their line against the wall by drilling in specially designed carabiners. One by one, they lowered themselves into the darkness.

Jerome was the last to descend into the hole. His

eyes drifted across the mass of squirming vines and decaying bodies throughout the atrium, then slid into the hole.

His feet hit the rocks below. Unclipping himself from the rope, he spun toward his men with his rifle drawn. The light embedded in the side of his helmet kicked on. With the beams of the team's flashlights working in tandem, Jerome could make out a long tunnel carved into the stone. He was about to give the order to move into the tunnel when Perez's voice came over the radio.

"Does anyone…" Static crackled in Jerome's helmet, cutting Perez off. "Buzz." The word broke through the static.

The pit in Jerome's stomach grew deeper.

"Do you…" Perez's voice broke through the static again.

"The static is too bad. Use hand signals," he commanded. None of his men seemed to respond, and he wondered if he was getting through at all.

His hand flew to his visor. Pushing the release button on the side, the mask fell away. The stale recycled oxygen in his suit was immediately replaced with the acrid stench of rot. The malodor filled his nose, making his eyes water. Forcing back a gag, he cleared his throat. "Radios are shot down here. Use hand signals."

He grabbed his facemask and swung it into place but stopped short of securing it. He could hear it now. There was a subtle buzzing noise coming from deeper in the tunnel. The sound rose and fell in a steady rhythm, like the breaths of a sleeping giant.

Jerome squeezed his eyes shut and clicked his mask into place. Recycled air flooded his system, but the stench of death still lingered.

The men moved in unison, maintaining as much discipline and proper dispersion as they could in these tight confines. Jerome moved in the middle of the pack. Every few seconds, he tried to radio the Vertibird that should be hovering overhead. Ideally, he would send them their video feed and the pilots could forward it on to base, but nothing was getting through these walls.

The buzzing noise grew louder with every meter. What had previously seemed like slow, laborious breaths grew in speed. It reminded Jerome of an asthma attack. The buzzing exploded into fits of furious noise that rapidly cut out, only to start again a moment later. The pattern seemed to speed up as they approached, the noise rising into a crescendo through the audio filters in their helmets. Jerome could feel the rapid vibrations as it rolled through the rocks.

Ahead of them, the tunnel turned hard to the left. Killian was the first man around the corner. He immediately dropped to his knee and raised his rifle. The buzzing became an incessant, panicked cry. Killian recoiled from the noise, stumbling backward against the wall behind him. His hands flew instinctually to his head as he attempted to cover his ears. He slid down the wall, screaming into his helmet.

Victor rushed forward and grabbed Killian by the shoulders. He dragged the man back around the corner. Releasing the clasp on Killian's facemask, Victor pulled it away.

Jerome's blood ran cold. Blood gushed from Killian's eyes and nose, forming rivers across his face. The young private's eyes rolled into the back of his head and his body began shaking.

Victor ripped off his own mask. "Fuck! What do we do?" he cried.

Every bit of Jerome's training told him to keep his mask in place, but he had to direct his men. He pulled his mask off. "Perez. Myers. Get around the corner and eliminate whatever is over there. Henry." He waited for the soldier to look up at him. "Drag him back fifty feet, then join us on our push forward.

We have to eliminate the threat before we can help him." Jerome realized he was screaming to be heard above the buzzing. He returned his mask to its place without waiting for an acknowledgment from Victor Henry. Turning his attention to the other two men, he nodded.

In one smooth motion, the three men rounded the corner and rushed forward.

The tunnel opened before them into a cavernous room. Enormous stalagmites stretched from the ground like jagged fingers toward a ceiling hundreds of feet above them. Thick, red vines wrapped themselves around them, riding the slowly developing features toward the sky. All around them, the vines slithered like a pit of vipers desperately seeking out their prey.

Jerome's eyes ran across the vines, and he realized they all led back to the center of the room. Jerking his head to the right, he saw it.

An amorphous growth wrapped in veins sprouted from within the tangle of vines. It throbbed in rapid succession, beating like a panicked heart. The buzzing emanated from the top of the growth, where a series of bright yellow tentacles vibrated spastically.

"What the..." Jerome's words trailed off as the

buzzing grew even louder. Beside him, Perez dropped to his knees and grabbed his head. The Sergeant squirmed on the ground, his legs kicking violently.

Jerome raised his rifle with the intention of shooting the heart-like mass when something yanked his left leg out from under him. He crashed to the floor, his head smashing into a rock and dazing him. If it hadn't been for his helmet, the impact probably would have cracked his skull. He shook away the fog clouding his brain and looked down.

One of the red vines was draped around his ankle. Slowly, it retracted toward the heart in the center of the room, dragging him across the ground. His eyes stretched open wide. He kicked at the vine with his free foot, but it had no effect. The vine wrapped tighter, denting the armor around his leg. A bolt of pain shot through him as he felt his bones splintering from the pressure.

Gunfire erupted from behind him. The growth in the center of the room wiggled with the impact of each bullet. Spouts of red fluid gushed from the holes.

The yellow tentacles vibrated faster, their buzzing now in a symphony that threatened to burst Jerome's ear drums. He looked back to see Myers and Henry moving forward, emptying their magazines into whatever this thing was. There was a brief pause in the gunfire as both men dropped their magazines and began reloading. Jerome watched in horror as the vines snaked their way across the floor. When they were within a few feet of Victor Henry, they raised up, preparing to strike.

Victor noticed it too late. He tried to step back, but one of the vines shot forward with unbelievable speed. It punched through the armor on his thigh and came out the other side. Victor screamed in pain, his cries muffled by his facemask. He tried to yank his leg away from the vine but lost his balance and collapsed to the floor. In a bout of manic fear, he swatted at the vine like it was a common mosquito. The vine ignored his strikes. It wrapped around his leg, constricting until the crunch of bone could be heard above the chaos.

Myers reloaded his rifle and aimed it at the vine. He squeezed off a burst and watched as the rounds chewed through the vine. He fired again and again. No matter how many times he shot it, the thing wouldn't release its hold on Victor's leg. Another vine shot out and wrapped itself around Victor's right arm. Then another stabbed itself through his right leg. Victor shook violently on the ground, desperately trying to pull himself away from the vines.

In unison, the vines tightened and pulled.

Jerome and Myers could do nothing but watch in horror as the vines ripped off the Private's legs and right arm. Fountains of blood spurted from the open wounds as the vines retreated into the tangle of tentacles with their prize.

Victor's breathing grew more rapid for a few seconds before ceasing all together.

Jerome's attention drifted from Victor's lifeless body to Perez. The soldier lay sprawled across the ground. Blood coated his visor, telling Jerome that his right-hand man was dead.

A bolt of pain shot up his leg, pulling him back to his own predicament. He was still being dragged across the floor toward the center of the room. His hands flew to his facemask and ripped it away.

"Myers! Run!" he screamed.

Myers stood there, subtly shaking his head. His gaze moved across his fallen comrades, pausing long enough to watch Perez's lifeless corpse disappear into a mass of vines.

"You have to warn the colony!" Jerome screamed. "That's an order!"

At the word 'order,' Myers' posture stiffened

slightly. He nodded at his Captain. Turning away from the massacre, he sprinted toward the tunnel and disappeared from view.

Jerome felt another of the tentacles worming its way across his torso. He fought the urge to vomit and dug into a box attached to his left hip. Retrieving a grenade, he ripped the safety pin out and pressed the button. It released a loud screech then began beeping. The beeps grew more rapid with every passing moment. Using the last of his strength, he threw the grenade toward the heart in the center of the room.

The vines were moving faster now. They slithered across his body, wrapping around him. They pulled him across the ground and into the mess of vines. The smaller ones climbed into his nostrils, inching their way toward his brain. He opened his mouth to scream, only for the vines to rush in. Gagging as they slid down his throat, he silently begged for death.

He heard the distant boom from his grenade. Part of him expected the vines to stop moving, but they didn't. They continued constricting until they forced the air from his lungs. The bones in his spine popped under the pressure. Darkness encroached at the corners of his vision until the world faded to black.

Myers sprinted along the hallway. The

cacophonous roar of a grenade going off rumbled along the rock walls around him. He reached the hole in the floor and hooked himself to his rope. Pressing a button on his waistband, a machine whirled to life, propelling him up the rope with growing speed.

In the atrium, the vines swung around the room wildly. The half-rotten corpses of the Mormons came apart, decorating the room in gore. Ignoring the horrific scene, Myers sprinted through the room and didn't stop until he exploded through the doorway, exiting Fort Joseph Smith.

He reached for his facemask but froze with his fingers on the release.

All around him, the red tentacles pushed their way through cracks in the ground. They continued rising into the air, darkening the sky.

Myers watched helplessly as massive vines wrapped themselves around the Vertibird and crushed it like a soda can. His heartbeat quickened as more vines climbed the ramp toward him.

Drawing his pistol from its holster, he pressed the barrel to his temple. He squeezed his eyes shut and exhaled slowly. The world around him fell silent.

As he died, he listened to the beating heart of Colony Three.

THE END

Publisher's Note

Going into this anthology, I had no idea what I was doing. To be quite honest, I really still don't, I just hope I'm winging it well enough that it doesn't show *too* often. I have so many people to be thankful for throughout this process, but that would simply take too much time, and as you've seen… Time flies. So, I just want to extend my gratitude to the following authors and give you a little fun fact about them you won't find anywhere else. This anthology also wouldn't be possible without the best BETA team there is, so to Alison H, Alison O., Ashley, Katie, Sherri, and Jessie, thank you…you are just as important to the writing world as us authors.

Update: Since finishing this anthology, formatting has become my new living nightmare. Between myself, Timothy King and William Joseph we have used FIVE different formatting programs. We have all spent COUNTLESS hours and sleepless nights trying to properly format this file to no avail. We've tried at least 70 files at this point trying to get it right. At the time I'm writing this, the book releases in TEN days so this is my final attempt at appeasing the formatting gods into cooperating with us. I'm desperate at this point.

Jared Grace 1800's

I've been blessed to call Jared a friend for a while now. We've attempted to collaborate for a few events in the past and life has other plans. He's always been an incredible backing and support for myself and my work and plans so it's only right that I extended the same to him. As another New England native, I am thrilled to include him in this lineup and as the headliner for the entire story.

Fun fact: He can often be found lapping syrup off the maple trees during his barefoot hikes through the New Hampshire forests at 3 in the morning. He claims it cures insurmountable levels of not giving a single fuck ever.

DE McCluskey 1900-1920's

The US has Burger King but Liverpool is the truly lucky bunch having the chicken king. Dave is a truly great guy who I've been more than blessed to call a friend for quite a while now. He's a little quirky but he's like everyone's fun uncle. His writing has been such an inspiration to me, pressing me to step beyond my comforts and put my creative limits and boundaries to the test.

Fun fact: He can often be found creating custom cheeses from things like belly button lint, baby boogers and the little dribbles after he pees because he doesn't shake twice. He truly gets enjoyment out of seeing other's faces when he presents it on charcuterie boards at fancy gatherings that he wasn't even invited to in the first place.

D.L Winchester 1940-1960's

I had a story lined up for this time period originally and unfortunately the author had to drop out for personal reasons. I put out an author call VERY last minute and D.L replied with such an incredible story I couldn't help myself. I didn't even want to wait until the deadline, I knew this would be the story I'd be including. He's been incredibly thorough, professional and helpful in the process leading up to this release since then and I look forward to seeing more of his work in the future.

Fun fact: He once tried to open a museum dedicated to the dust bunnies he sculpted spending all those years in his mother's basement. To take it a step further, he even crafted miniature leashes for these benign creatures and takes them on strolls through his neighborhood on brisk Sunday mornings.

David Hardy 1960-1970's

David was one of the first people I considered a friend once I stepped into the bookish world. Since then, he's just been a nagging pain in my ass sending me repulsive videos of hotdogs and terrible foods. But he's also been an immensely great supporter and friend beyond just books. The conversations David and I have had, have had a profound impact on my life opening my mind to new thoughts and curiosities.

Fun fact: He tried going to space to offer the aliens glizzys and mayo but they banned him from ever returning, he now dedicates his time to sending me shitty videos solely to piss me off.

Brennan LaFaro 1970-1980's

I had the pleasure of meeting Brennan in the summer of 2024 when I hosted the Authors Against Abuse expo. Brennan was a lovely addition to our lineup and he's been a very caring and supportive part of my tribe since then. As a New England native having him along for the ride for this anthology has been an honor.

Fun fact: He showed up for open tryouts for the New York Yankees requesting the position of designated ass wiper for the team mascot. His enthusiasm for the position scared the entire team to the point they got a no contact order against him. He is now said to be a Boston Red Sox fan but only to hide his true identity.

Rob Bilodeau - 1990 - 2000's

This story holds a special place in my heart. It is my uncle's debut piece that I damn near begged him to finally dip his toes in the water and submit. Having a family member who not only reads the same genre as you, but who will write alongside you is a rare experience that I am beyond grateful for. To be able to showcase his work to the world for the first time is a dream come true.

Fun Fact : He works on an ambulance, but it is only because the blinky lights and the funny noises entertain his feeble mind. When he's not at work he's usually watching the bubbles float to the top in some awful tasting beer.

William Joseph 2000-2020's

William very quickly became a big part of my day to day life both in a literary sense and just that as a friend. He's shown me ferocious loyalty, kindness and so much support. He refuses to let me give up or fail and for that I am eternally grateful. I'd like to think it is mutual. This anthology wouldn't feel right if he weren't included.

Fun fact: William makes being a "jersey boy" his entire personality. He can be seen at every single Jersey Shore fan party and signing and once collected 3 q-tips that Ronnie had left in a port-a-potty in Seaside Heights.

Timothy King 3000's

Tim and I have kinda "grown up" together in the bookish world. We wrote and released our debuts around the same time as one another and being able to see his work flourish and take off is one of life's greatest joys for me. His writing touches on topics that demand your respect and attention and I sincerely trust any input he gives me towards any work I've done.

Fun Fact: Tim had to convince his beautiful wife, Rhianna to marry him still once she found out he only went after her thinking she was the singer and that he has a major kink for masked men... particularly rabbits.

Jared Grace

Jared Grace is the author of *Isolation*, his well-received debut horror novel that's already making waves as a finalist for the Indie Ink Awards 2024 in a variety of categories. Born just south of Boston, Massachusetts, Jared now calls the scenic White Mountains of New Hampshire home, where he spends his days hiking trails, chasing his muse, researching paranormal events, and devouring books from his favorite authors across a wide range of genres.

When he's not working on his next spine-tingling tale, Jared is busy being a proud dad to his two incredible kids, Jordan and Wyatt, who keep him equally terrified and inspired (but in the best way).

After a brief pit stop at Boston College, Jared earned not one, but two bachelor's degrees—English and history—from Southern New Hampshire University in 2014.

Jared's love for history, nature, travel, and the supernatural seeps into his stories, making them equal parts eerie, thought-provoking, and unputdownable. Whether he's digging into spooky folklore or climbing a mountain, Jared finds inspiration everywhere—especially in the things that go bump in the night.

You can follow Jared at the following locations:

AuthorJaredg.com
Facebook–Author Jared Grace
https://www.facebook.com/profile.php?id=61552742355013
TikTok–AuthorJaredG https://www.tiktok.com/@jaredgrace61
Instagram–Paranormaljared
https://www.instagram.com/paranormaljared/
Bluesky–AuthorJaredG AuthorJaredG (@authorjaredg.bsky.social) — Bluesky
Amazon https://a.co/d/iTp0aV3

DE McCluskey

Born in the UK long before school was invented, Dave began life in a music shop selling guitars and drums and playing in local bands around the Liverpool music scene. When fame and fortune, and rock god status, proved elusive, he decided to waste many years of his life playing around with computers.

He quickly bored of these and decided to write novels in his 30s. He writes as DE McCluskey, mostly in the genre of horror (mainstream, extreme, and comedy), although he has been known to dabble in thrillers, romance, science fiction, fantasy, and also children's books. Ever since, the riches, fame, and the fortune, has continued to elude him.

Find him lurking on Facebook and all the other crappy social media outlets.

Laura Bilodeau

Laura is a 28-year-old single mom to two boys from literally the middle of nowhere in the northeast corner of Connecticut. She is the author of Defeating the Moose, Dr. Grinsaw and Punkin Head's Revenge. She has also appeared in two other anthologies prior to this one. She thrives on daily naps and Coca Cola.

You can find her primarily on:
Facebook: @ Laura Bilodeau Author
But also TikTok: @ lit.me.up
Or by email Bilodeau.Laura96@gmail.com

D.L. Winchester

D.L. Winchester lives in the foothills of southern Appalachia. A former mortician, his work searches the darkness to find tales worth telling. He is the author of over three hundred obituaries, numerous short stories, the novella *The Screaming House*, and the collections *Shadows of Appalachia* and *A Terrible Place and Other Flashes of Horror*.

D.L. also serves as the President and Associate Editor of Undertaker Books, an independent horror publisher. In his spare time, he can be found searching for inspiration in the world around him and helping his wife try to keep their children from becoming the next generation of horror villains.

David Hardy

Hello Fleshbags,

I'm a self proclaimed Horror Aficionado, Horror Author who loves any and all things Macabre. If I'm not writing, I'm geeking out on space stuff or watching Horror Movies. I can spend hours talking about the universe, or how horror has shaped the entertainment industry as we know it. I have a deep rooted love of anything zombies thanks to the king Mr. George Romero.

Outside of the fascinating deplorable world that is my imagination, I......well.......I don't really know cause my imagination is my world. If it involves go fast automobiles, gearhead/petrolhead, dark disturbing horror, or space, we will probably get a long just great.

Brennan LaFaro

Brennan LaFaro is a music teacher by day, horror writer by night, living in southeastern Massachusetts with his wife, two sons, and his hounds. He is the author of the Slattery Falls trilogy, the Buzzard's Edge Saga, as well as Illusions of Isolation and Last Stay. You can read his short fiction in various anthologies and find him on Twitter at @brennanlafaro or at www.brennanlafaro.com.

Rob Bilodeau

Rob is a nightwalker from the Quiet Corner of Connecticut, and a lifelong horror fan. This is his first foray into writing.

William Joseph

William Joseph is an exciting Horror, Paranormal, and Psychological Thriller writer from New Jersey, USA. He loves to draw the reader into believable worlds, creating everyday characters the readers can relate and connect with, and then forcing them to face their deepest and darkest fears. William Joseph's writing has been detailed as twisted, dark, terrifying, raw, and emotional.

Timothy King

Timothy King is an adult horror author who enjoys delving into the complexities of human nature. When he is not writing spine-chilling tales, he is spending time with his wife and kids in beautiful Tampa, Florida.

You can find him on Facebook, Tiktok or by emailing him at:

Timothykingauthor@gmail.com

If you enjoyed this book, please consider leaving a review on Amazon or Goodreads!